shadow chaser

the shadow agency
book two

Christy Barritt

Copyright © 2024 by Christy Barritt

All rights reserved.

No part of this book may be reproduced in any form or by any electronic or mechanical means, including information storage and retrieval systems, without written permission from the author, except for the use of brief quotations in a book review.

one

A SMOKY SCENT roused Emily Rankin from a deep sleep.

She pulled one eye open, then the other.

She was still in her bed, she realized. Darkness surrounded her. She still wore her pale pink pajamas.

Had she been having a dream? A dream about a bonfire maybe?

She sniffed again then sat up with a start.

This was no dream.

She really smelled smoke right now.

She blinked as she glanced around her room. Haze surrounded her.

Smoke, she realized. Smoke filled her bedroom, hovering near the ceiling.

Panic raced through her.

Bree . . .

She had to check on her daughter.

Emily threw off her duvet cover. Snatching the sweater from the foot of her bed, she tugged it on as she rushed toward the hallway.

As soon as she opened the door, flames shot inside, reaching out to grab her.

A wall of heat blasted her face.

Her eyes burned. Coughs racked her body. The hair on her arms singed.

She slammed the door before the blaze could reach her.

Her house was on fire. Not *just* on fire. It was engulfed and almost completely consumed, she realized as she heard the wood frame crackling.

Her heart pounded in her ears as her thoughts raced.

Bree! She had to help her daughter.

The six-year-old slept in the room next to Emily's.

But the hallway was blocked by flames. She would have to get to her another way.

Wasting no more time, Emily grabbed the cell from her nightstand, rushed to her bedroom window, and shoved it open. She scrambled outside, her bare feet hitting the prickly mulch.

She rushed to the window beside hers and peered inside.

Thick, black smoke curled through her daughter's room. The billows were so heavy she couldn't even see any of the furniture. Not the bed, the dresser, the nightstand.

Not her daughter.

Nothing.

Emily banged furiously on the window. "Bree! Bree! Can you hear me?"

It was no use. Emily couldn't see anything. She heard no response.

She swung her gaze around, looking for something to break the glass.

She grabbed a terracotta flowerpot from the porch and slammed it into the window.

The glass shattered, and fire shot outside.

The force threw Emily backward onto the grass behind her.

Flames burst from the house in all directions.

Adrenaline propelled her back to her feet. Back to the window.

Her desperate gaze roamed her daughter's bedroom.

Flames consumed it—all of it. There was no way anyone inside could have survived.

A wail began down deep inside her chest. "Bree! No, no, no . . . !"

She lifted her phone to call 911. Before she could, a text message filled her screen.

> Your daughter is safe—for now. Tell the police and she'll die.

Wait . . . what? Someone had taken her daughter and set her house on fire? Then this person had left Emily there to die.

The world began to spin around her.

———

NORMALLY, Austin Greenwich went into assignments more prepared. But this newest one had been thrown at him at the last minute. He'd completed his last mission at midnight when he'd gotten the text from his boss to hop on a plane.

Wasting no time, Austin left Louisiana, where he'd helped take down a bayou mob king. Now, bright and early this morning, he was in Pennsylvania's Amish country.

He'd landed in Harrisburg and rented a car. He had a meeting at a café in Lancaster.

He knew the important talking points: single mom, house fire, missing child.

It sounded like a case for the FBI, not the Shadow Agency. But he'd hear out the woman who wanted to hire them. Larchmont had given Austin the freedom to either take or reject this case.

All he knew about this woman was that her name was Emily.

Emily . . . a pretty name. He'd known an Emily once.

She was someone Austin would never forget.

Even though he should. Even though he'd *tried*.

He sighed and glanced at the town around him.

He'd always found Lancaster and the Amish living in the area fascinating. Sometimes he thought the simpler way of life would be nice. His life had more than its fair share of complications.

He touched the scars on his arm as memories pummeled him.

Speaking of the Amish . . . Emily seemed like it could be an Amish name. Was the woman he was meeting with Pennsylvania Dutch? From what he knew, the Amish didn't seem like the type who'd hire him. But he'd been wrong before.

He found a parking space down the street, left his car there, and then headed toward the café.

He arrived right on time.

He stepped into the quaint restaurant with its yellow awning and colorful pansies springing from window boxes out front. Inside, the scent of bacon and freshly baked bread tantalized his senses.

Austin's stomach immediately rumbled. Maybe it would be good to get something to eat. He'd had a snack on the airplane, but it hadn't been enough to hold him over.

He paused inside and glanced across the space. Families filled most of the booths. A man and woman sat together, leaning close across the table. Three women chatted at another table.

His gaze stopped on a woman sitting alone at a corner booth, her back toward him.

That had to be Emily.

He squared his shoulders and smoothed a hand over his black T-shirt in a last-ditch effort to look professional.

Then he strode across the café and slid into the booth across from her. He already had the dialogue worked out, verbiage that would be sure to impress Larchmont.

A new leadership position within the organization was close enough to touch.

But as soon as he saw the woman's face, everything he had planned slipped from his mind.

"Emily?" he rushed.

Her eyes widened. "Austin?"

They stared at each other.

No . . . it couldn't be.

The universe wasn't small.

Coincidences like this didn't happen.

There had to be some mistake.

Yet here she was. The Emily from his past. The Emily with honey-blonde hair, girl-next-door features, and stunning green eyes.

She stared at him from the other side of the table, as beautiful as ever—despite the bandage on her arm and her oversized clothing.

Austin had been sure their paths would never cross again.

"What are you doing here?" she rushed.

"What are *you* doing here?" he countered.

That wasn't what he should have said. He should tell her how he thought about her all the time for the past seven years. How what had happened between them had been a mistake. How he'd wished he could go back and change things.

But none of those sentiments left his lips. Instead, he sat there dumbfounded.

"I'm meeting someone here." Emily raised her head and pulled her shoulders back, an invisible wall shooting up around her.

Austin stared at her. "So am I."

They glared at each other another moment.

Glared? Why was he glaring at her? She'd done nothing wrong.

It was just that seeing her . . . it brought back so many memories.

Memories he wanted to forget. Regrets, really.

Emily shook her head and started to stand. "I don't know what's going on here, but this must be a mistake."

Austin quickly stood also, still trying to put everything together. "You're right. This has to be a mistake. Because the two of us . . . we're not meeting each other, right? It must be another Emily . . ."

He looked around, but there was no one else sitting at a table alone.

Emily stared at him. "You're supposed to be meeting an Emily? Here? Right now?" She shook her head, her eyes closing with disappointment. "I wouldn't have purposefully asked to meet with you."

Austin had so many questions. But before he could ask any of them, she hurried toward the door.

Austin couldn't let her leave. He had an assignment to do.

He followed her through the café. She didn't slow down as she pushed through the door and stepped outside. Instead, she dashed toward the street corner, clearly in a hurry to get away from him.

"Emily . . . wait!"

She paused but didn't turn back toward him.

At least it was a start.

He rushed to catch up.

Just as he did, an SUV screeched to a halt across the street.

As Austin turned toward the vehicle, gunfire cut through the air.

two

EMILY FROZE, unsure what was happening.

More bullets sliced through the air. People screamed. The pedestrians around them scattered.

Austin grabbed her arms and jerked her behind a car parked at the street.

Her pulse quickened. That couldn't be right. Things like this didn't happen in real life. Only on TV or to other people.

Yet she knew that wasn't true.

As a psychologist, she worked with people all the time who'd been through the unimaginable.

Now the unimaginable was happening to her.

She glanced around, searching for more details. Trying to make sense of things. To come up with a survival plan.

Austin crouched over her, his body between her and the gunman. His jean jacket brushed her arms. His piney scent filled her nose.

She pushed away the memories. Wished he didn't have to be so close.

Shattered glass lay on the sidewalk by a nearby storefront. People cowered behind walls and doorways. A man held his shoulder as he leaned against the door of a quilt shop.

He'd been shot, Emily realized.

She started to rise. To rush toward him. To offer help.

But Austin kept an iron grip on her arm. "Stay down! It's still not safe."

Her heart throbbed in her ears, mixed with ringing from the gunfire. All of it made her head swirl.

Were these guys not done shooting? Her blood went cold at the thought.

Austin released her arm, reached beneath his jacket, and pulled out a . . . gun.

He had a gun also?

Her heart thrummed even harder.

As he rose up from behind the car, another squeal sounded.

"They're leaving," Austin muttered.

Emily's chest muscles loosened just slightly.

Austin placed a hand on her shoulder and kept her low another moment.

Then he rose. Grabbed her arm. Pulled her to her feet. "We need to get out of here."

"Shouldn't we wait for the police?" Panic laced her voice.

Leaving seemed like a terrible idea. People around her needed help. As a psychologist, she could offer a listening ear. Help keep people calm until paramedics arrived.

"Your safety is more urgent," he barked.

Her safety?

The reality of his statement hit her. "Wait . . . you think those gunmen were shooting at *me*?"

Austin cast her a skeptical glance, with one eye squinted, piercing her with a knowing look. "That's my assumption."

"You're the one with the gun," Emily reminded him. "Certainly, you have enemies also. Maybe those guys were targeting you."

He shoved his gun back into the holster beneath his jacket. Then he took her arm and led her away.

"Wait . . . I don't even know that I want to hire you."

"We can't discuss that out here. It will be hard for you to hire me if you're dead."

His words left her startled—no doubt, the effect he wanted.

Emily still wasn't sure leaving the scene was the right choice.

Yet she didn't have any better ideas.

So she let the man who'd broken her heart lead her away.

But she dreaded the conversations they needed to have . . . especially the one he would least expect.

———

AUSTIN HAD to set his emotions aside. Right now, all that mattered was getting Emily to safety.

Then they could talk.

But her question had been valid. He wasn't certain if those gunmen had been after her or him. He certainly had his fair share of enemies . . . namely, Brigitta Johansson and her minions. The woman—a terrorist who presented herself as a business professional—had promised to find him and kill him.

Although Carlos Baudouin had now moved up on his list.

The mob boss was officially behind bars, but he had men who would like nothing more than to exact revenge on Austin. In fact, Carlos had vowed to order his men to do just that.

Austin needed to hear more of Emily's story before he made any determinations.

He ushered her to the electric-blue Mustang convertible he'd rented.

Not exactly low profile, but that couldn't be helped now.

Just as sirens began to wail in the distance, he sped away.

He knew security cameras were probably perched atop the doors of nearby businesses. He knew the police would probably track him down as a witness. There would be questions, and his actions right now would seem suspicious.

But he needed to get Emily to safety.

Depending on the intricacies of the case, Austin could either go to the police later to explain his side of the story. Or Larchmont, his boss, could make any security footage with Austin's image disappear.

His boss had the strange ability to pull strings like that. He had an unusual amount of connections in the government. Those connections had been important for the covert missions Austin had been on. Covering their tracks had been essential.

Austin headed out of town, the top to the car

down—something he could now see was a mistake. But when he'd pulled up to meet Emily, he'd had no idea of the turn of events about to unfold.

The wind hit them, making it hard to talk.

But maybe that was better.

He needed to get his thoughts under control first. He hadn't expected to see Emily. Hadn't expected this danger.

What about the fire? The missing girl? How did all this connect?

He wove through the quaint streets of Lancaster, past the historic storefronts and a large, steepled church. Several minutes later, the town was in his rearview mirror, and wide-open country spaces replaced the bustling retail area.

As he skirted around a horse and buggy on the road in front of him, he glanced beside him. Saw Emily's pale face. Saw her trembling hands as she gripped the armrest.

The woman was terrified, as anyone would be in a situation like this.

When he'd first seen Emily in the café and realized she was his assignment, Austin had been instantly certain he'd walk away from this case.

Not because he was angry with her. To be truthful, he wanted to walk away because being around her would make him too vulnerable. It would be too easy to fall for the woman all over again.

Given Austin's line of work and his past, he couldn't afford to do that.

Finally, he turned onto a long dirt road, pulled onto the grass at the edge, and put the vehicle in Park. Seedlings had just begun to pop up in the fields surrounding them. It was April, and everything felt fresh and new.

But not being with Emily.

Being with Emily was a brutal reminder of his past.

He swallowed hard as he turned to her. "I heard you wanted to hire us."

He waited to hear what Emily had to say.

three

EMILY LET OUT A SHALLOW, incredulous breath as she stared at Austin. "*That's* what you're going to lead with?"

The audacity of this man.

The two of them hadn't seen each other for seven years, and *that* was how he wanted to start the conversation?

Besides, Emily still wasn't sure what Austin was doing here. Or what she was doing with him. Or what had just happened.

To be truthful, nothing made sense.

But logic and timing and coincidences didn't matter right now. Only Bree.

"Why are you even here?" Emily turned to observe him.

She soaked in his light-brown hair, cut short on the sides but left long on top. His broad frame. His piercing brown eyes.

"I'm here because I'm supposed to meet a client named Emily about a job." Austin crossed his arms and stared at her. "I'm guessing you're that Emily."

Her bad mood continued to darken. "You're telling me you work for the Shadow Agency?"

His jaw twitched. "I do."

"I didn't know *you* worked for them. Otherwise, I would have investigated other options." She crossed her arms too, furious with herself that she hadn't done more research.

Austin sighed and ran a hand through his thick hair. But he didn't argue. Certainly, he couldn't deny her words.

From the moment they'd first met seven years ago, Emily had thought he was handsome. Brooding. Mysterious.

Off-limits.

All those things, when combined with her circumstances at that moment, had led Emily to make a very bad mistake.

Well, the mistake wasn't *all* terrible. Good had come out of it. But still . . .

She swallowed hard, remembering that she didn't

believe in coincidences. Maybe Austin's sudden appearance in her life had a purpose. Maybe God had even ordained it.

Since moving to Lancaster, she'd begun going to church.

Her whole life she'd been searching for something. Until recently, she didn't know it was God.

Throughout her higher education, the idea of God had been scoffed at. She'd had the same attitude. She hadn't wanted to believe there was a Higher Power at work.

But the walls around her heart had come down as she learned more. As she researched for herself. As she decided to give faith a try.

Becoming a Christian had changed her whole life.

Besides, her past with Austin didn't matter right now.

Only Bree.

The thought of her daughter caused a swirl of nausea followed by the tightening of her muscles. She hadn't known such deep emotional pain and worry until this happened.

She turned back to Austin, determined to stay focused only on what was important. "Look, I'm not here to talk about our history together. I'm not really sure you're the person I want to talk to at all. Maybe another agent should take this job. But the fact of the matter is my daughter was kidnapped, and I'll do whatever it takes to get her back."

"How did you even hear about us?" He observed her a moment.

"A man showed up at the scene of the fire. He handed me a card and said I should call. That he could help."

"Was his name Alan Larchmont?"

Emily shrugged. "I'm not sure. I didn't ask. As quickly as he appeared, he was gone. But he said you guys were the best. That's why I called . . . that and desperation."

Austin drew in a long, deep breath as if gathering his thoughts. "Okay. I still have more questions but, for now, let's talk about your daughter. Tell me what happened."

Emily swallowed hard as she wondered how much she should say. The story was way more complicated than Austin would ever realize. But she didn't need to get into all of those details right now.

However, she also knew she couldn't go to the police. The kidnappers had said they'd kill Bree if she did.

So that left her with Austin. She didn't have time to track down anyone else who might be able to help.

"Last night, someone set the house I've been renting on fire." Emily rubbed her arm where a cut throbbed. She'd sliced open her forearm at some point while trying to reach Bree.

"Go on."

"I tried to rescue Bree. I tried to get into her room but . . . the fire was so strong . . ." Her voice caught, and she rubbed her throat. It felt sore and raw from crying so much.

"You thought your daughter was inside?" Austin asked, his voice low and quiet.

Emily nodded. "I assumed she was in her bed sleeping. That's where she should have been. I panicked, and I tried to get through the window but . . ."

She held up her arm to show him her injury.

"I wanted to try again, but the flames . . . they consumed the house so quickly. The fire just ate everything in its path. I couldn't get inside her room."

"Then what?" His intense gaze remained on her.

"Then I got a text. The sender said Bree wasn't in the house. Said I shouldn't tell the cops. And if I did . . . she would be killed." She swallowed hard. "Firefighters arrived a few minutes later and put out the flames."

"And your daughter really wasn't in the house?"

"No. She wasn't there. Someone took her." Her voice cracked.

Austin sucked in a breath. "Someone took her and then set the house on fire . . ."

Emily nodded, somber at the realization. "I think someone meant for me to die, but I woke up just in time." Her gaze caught with his. "You have to help me get her back. Please. I'll do anything."

AUSTIN STARED AT EMILY, questions circling in his mind.

She was clearly upset. She didn't make any sounds, but moisture flowed down her cheeks and she rubbed her throat.

He couldn't even imagine what she was going through.

He observed her another moment.

Emily had a baby. She'd settled down in Pennsylvania, of all places. This wasn't the kind of location where he'd envisioned her living.

Then again, Austin didn't really know her that well.

"Was it just you and Bree in the house?" He still needed more information.

Emily used the back of her hand to wipe her tears and nodded quickly. Her voice sounded strained as she said, "Just the two of us."

Where had her husband been? Where was he now? Was he still in the picture?

Austin glanced at Emily's hand but didn't see a wedding ring, which was strange because she seemed like the marrying type.

That was exactly what had made her so dangerous to his heart all those years ago.

Emily wasn't like the other women Austin had been with. However, she'd said she wanted to throw caution to the wind.

He'd asked her if she was sure.

She'd insisted she had never been so sure of anything.

"Could your husband have done this?" In many situations like this, that was the most likely scenario. Cops always looked to relatives first.

Her gaze clouded. "He's dead."

She was a widow. He hadn't expected that. "I'm sorry."

Emily seemed to ignore his statement as her gaze locked with his. "So will you help me? With every second that passes, Bree could be slipping farther away."

"Is the FBI involved?" Austin needed to get a few more facts first. Needed to make sure he was thinking with his head not his heart.

"No." Her voice cracked. "I can't involve them. You remember what that text said. The kidnapper would kill her if I told the cops."

His eyes widened. "What kind of game is this person playing?"

Her gaze looked empty as she shrugged. "I have no idea. I wish I knew. But I didn't feel like I had any choice but to obey. I can't let anything happen to her, Austin. That's why I called you guys. I don't have a lot of money. But I'll figure out—"

He raised to hand to stop her thoughts. "Let's not worry about money right now."

Austin wasn't sure how Larchmont would feel about his statement, but Austin knew it was the right thing to do. He couldn't walk away from this, not if Emily needed him. And not with a little girl's life on the line.

Some things were more important than money.

He turned back to Emily, studying the grief on her face. He didn't want to beat around the bush. No, he had to be upfront about the reality of what would happen next.

"I'll need to see that text, figure out if we can trace it," he said. "In the meantime, tell me about Bree."

She reached into her pocket and pulled out what appeared to be a school photo. The girl in the picture made him suck in a breath.

She was beautiful with her light honey-blonde hair, freckles, and green eyes that glinted with mischief.

"After the fire was extinguished, I grabbed this from my car." Emily sounded hoarse as she said the words. "That's Bree. She loves adventures and exploring. She thinks she's always right. But she also loves reading and doing arts and crafts, and if someone she cares about is crying, she's the first one to cry with them."

"She sounds like a remarkable girl."

Emily smiled. "She is."

"Emily . . . you do realize that if I look for your little girl, the two of us will need to work together. Are you okay with that?"

She hesitated before nodding. "If that's what I have to do. I'll do whatever it takes to find her. The man I spoke with at the Shadow Agency said he was sending one of his best. I guess that's you. I can set my personal feelings aside."

Austin's throat squeezed with emotion, but he nodded. "I'm good at what I do."

"Then, yes, I'm okay working with you. Like I said, I'd do anything to get Bree back."

Austin heard the subtext of her words. *I'd do anything to get her back . . . even work with you.*

He couldn't take offense to the statement because he understood her reasoning. If the roles were reversed, he'd feel the same way. Desperation realigned people's priorities.

Austin nodded, decision made. "I'll help you find her. But, first, I need you to take me to the scene."

Yes, desperation had even realigned his priorities.

Because he prayed now. All the time, for that matter.

When he'd hit rock bottom, he'd discovered God.

And now Austin didn't know what he would do without his faith.

Lord, give me wisdom now. And please keep this little girl safe.

four

EMILY GAVE Austin directions to the small farm where she'd been living. Mostly, she'd pointed and nudged him since her voice couldn't easily be heard over the wind in the convertible.

Austin offered to put the top up, but she insisted she was okay. There'd always been something she loved about riding in a convertible. Bree had begged her to buy one—preferably a pink one—but Emily had refused. Said it was too dangerous. And it was.

But danger seemed to fit Austin. Emily had sensed that from the moment they'd first met. It had been part of what intrigued her.

He didn't fit all the safe parameters she'd always kept around herself—parameters that had gotten her nowhere.

She sighed and reflected on last night.

Emily had stayed at the scene for several hours until a relief agency had put her up in a hotel for the night. They'd given her some clothes in a backpack and one hundred dollars cash.

She'd been in the hotel room long enough to take a shower and get the smoky scent off. She'd donned some clean—but ill-fitting—clothes. She'd changed the bandage paramedics had placed around her arm.

She'd fretted and worried and tried to pray. She'd watched her phone, hoping for more instructions. She'd nearly had a panic attack but had tried to use practices she taught others in therapy to keep the anxiety under control.

Nothing had worked.

Out of desperation, she'd called the number on the card a stranger had given her.

A mysterious stranger.

His appearance still didn't make sense. How had the man known about Bree? Why had he sought Emily out? How had he shown up when he did?

As she and Austin pulled up to the Amish-owned home where Emily had been living for the past two years, her thoughts jolted back to the present.

No, she wasn't Amish. But she loved the peace and quiet of the area. Loved the fresh air. The open spaces.

Austin parked the car and stepped out, slamming the door. His gaze fixated on the burned remains of the structure in the distance.

The small white house Emily had called home had stood a good mile off the road. Crops stretched in front of it on one side and woods on the other. The place was all rolling hills and fresh air.

And the sunsets were amazing . . . enough to make Emily forget the scent of the cow pasture that wafted toward the house when the wind shifted.

"This is where you lived?" Austin scanned the rest of the area—the old barn and livestock shed and root cellar.

Emily climbed out also and moved to stand by him. Tears pressed at her eyes when she saw the house.

Memories—terrible memories—of the previous night captured her thoughts.

Memories of awaking to smoke. Realizing she couldn't get to her daughter. Fearing she was dead.

The memories made her want to break down. To immerse herself in the sadness and panic threatening to consume her.

But she couldn't. Not now.

There would be time to deal with her emotions later. Maybe even to go through these remains and see if there was anything left. Photos? Jewelry? Toys?

It seemed doubtful. Plus, the fire inspector had told her it wasn't safe to go into the building. Not for at least forty-eight hours. Doing so wasn't even on her radar right now.

Emily cleared her throat, trying to pull herself together. She remembered that Austin had asked her about living here, that he sounded confused about how she'd ended up on an Amish farm.

"I saw an ad for this place, a small house in the country," she explained. "It seemed perfect for Bree and me."

Joseph—the home's owner—and his family lived about a half mile from here—close enough to be there if she needed anything but far enough away to give her privacy.

Had her former father-in-law hired the person who'd set her place on fire? The more she thought about it, the more it made sense.

She'd taken all the necessary precautions after moving, even going as far as to change her career and delete her social media accounts. She'd canceled her credit cards and only paid in cash.

She *should* have been untraceable.

"So you said this happened last night?" Austin glanced away from the house and at her again.

"That's right. I managed to grab my phone—I knew I'd need to call 911—but my wallet and everything else is gone." Emily's throat burned as she said the words.

"I'm sorry for the loss." He pointed to an old sedan with melted tires behind the house. "I guess that was yours?"

She nodded. "That's right. I'm sure it's totaled now."

As Austin paced closer, Emily stayed near him. Memories filled her—horrible memories. Memories of the panic and helplessness she'd felt. First, thinking her daughter was dead. Then getting that text and realizing Bree had been kidnapped.

Realizing the person who'd tried to kill her must be close. Must have been watching and realized she'd survived what had been meant to kill her. Realized he had to implement Plan B.

Emily closed her eyes, trying to find her equilibrium.

She wouldn't truly be able to find it again, not until Bree was back with her. She felt like she was living in a state of shock, like she was someone else and only going through motions of living.

Grief and trauma could cause a shell to form around people, making the rest of life feel like an out of body experience. Nothing seemed real, yet everything seemed all too real.

She knew that firsthand now.

"Do you have any idea who may have taken her?" Austin still stood there, his intense gaze on her.

Emily rubbed her throat as a raw, burning sensation spread up the inside. "I suspect it's the father of my deceased husband."

Something flickered in Austin's gaze. "Tell me more about your husband and his family."

Emily wrapped her arms over her chest, wishing she didn't have to tell this side of the story. "Paul died two and a half years ago. I was never a big fan of Conrad, his father—nor was Conrad a fan of mine. After Paul died, I decided Bree and I needed a change, so we left New York and came here. Conrad didn't like that. He wanted us to stay close to him so he could 'take care of us.'"

"You think Conrad went through all this trouble and almost killed you in order to get custody of his granddaughter?"

Emily swallowed hard and nodded. That sounded like the best possibility, especially considering that text. Especially considering the fact Conrad always got what he wanted.

Every holiday at his place. Every vacation with him.

He'd dictated Paul's schedule. Where Paul should live. How Emily should present herself as the wife of a wealthy businessman.

No thank you.

She knew her theory sounded crazy. But Austin didn't know Conrad. She knew the lengths the man would go through to get what he wanted. She'd seen it firsthand.

And the fact that her house had been set on fire . . . that couldn't be a coincidence either.

"That's right," she croaked. "I do. I really do."

———

AUSTIN STARED AT EMILY. There was something she wasn't telling him.

But what? If she was so desperate to find her daughter, why keep secrets?

He wasn't sure. But at least a better picture had formed in his mind.

Emily had been married. Her husband had died. Shortly after, Emily and Bree had fled and moved to the middle of nowhere.

There had to be more to that story. He felt certain of it.

"Did you have electricity out here?" Austin glanced around, looking for a powerline.

It sounded like a meaningless question, but he wondered if firefighters had identified what started the fire. If it was proven to be arson, there would be a lot of questions for Emily. There would be an investigation.

It might even be discovered that Bree had been taken.

"We did have electricity. Even though an Amish man owns this place, he doesn't expect his renters to live like he and his family do."

Austin grunted. He didn't know much about the Amish, but living without electricity seemed unnecessarily harder. But to each his own. It didn't bother him that others lived different lifestyles than his.

"I mean, if you think about it, other businesses the Amish own have electricity," Emily continued. "Amish-owned restaurants, for example, have lights and AC. Their businesses are a way they make money, so they make accommodations."

"When you explain it that way, it makes sense." Austin paused, still trying to form a complete picture. "Why did you pick this area to live?"

She shrugged. "It's quiet. Peaceful. Bree and I spend a lot of time together reading and making crafts and going on walks. It was a nice change of pace from the city."

Austin stared at her another moment. "Do you work?"

Maybe she was simply living off a life insurance policy. He wasn't really sure. But he didn't think so. Emily seemed like the type who liked to work and earn her keep.

"I used to work full time. I was a psychologist."

A psychologist. When they'd met all those years ago, she'd told him she'd just finished earning her master's degree at a Virginia university. That she was planning to get her doctorate next.

"That's great," he told her. "I'm glad all your hard work paid off."

Somehow the statement felt a little too intimate. Like too much of a reminder that they had a past together. Too much of a reminder that they'd once connected and cared for each other, no matter how brief it might have been.

Emily rubbed her neck as if soothing out a knot there. "I switched to part time after Bree was born. I wanted more time with her. But I'm not actually practicing right now," she quickly told him. "I've been working in a quilt shop while Bree is in school."

"Why did you stop?"

"I thought it would be too easy to track me down if I set up a practice here. Plus, my license is in New York."

Austin stepped closer to the house, wanting to see the charred remains better. Wanting to see where the fire had started. What might have been used as an accelerant.

He had some training in fire investigation. It had been one of the many skills he'd learned during his time in the military.

His leaders had wanted him to be prepared for anything.

He froze before he reached the remnants of the house.

Angled his ear toward the street.

Cast a glance over his shoulder.

"Austin?" Emily stared at him as if she were concerned.

He put a finger over his lips to motion for her to be quiet.

There was that sound again.

The sound of another vehicle coming down the gravel lane.

Since it was mostly the Amish out here, Austin couldn't see a reason anyone else would be coming this way in a motor vehicle—unless it was the police or fire department.

But he couldn't chance it.

They needed to hide just in case trouble had shown up.

five

EMILY STARED AT AUSTIN, startled at his reaction. However, she didn't have time to think about things for long.

He grabbed her arm. "You see that barn over there? Get behind it. Now."

"But—" She glanced at the barn, confusion gripping her.

Why did he suddenly seem alarmed?

Austin's gaze locked with hers, and his voice left no room for argument. "I'll explain later. For now, move."

With one last glance at him, Emily took off. She heard him running in the other direction. Heard his car engine start.

She reached the barn and ducked behind it. Then

she peered around the corner. Saw Austin moving his car behind a patch of trees in the distance.

What was the man doing?

Then she heard another sound.

The sound of a vehicle coming down the lane.

Who might it be? Firefighters coming to check out the scene again? The cops following them from the scene of the shooting?

And how had Austin heard the engine so much earlier than she did?

Her heart pounded in her ears as she waited.

She wished Austin was beside her. She felt safer when he was close.

After all, if he hadn't been there when those men fired those bullets, she might not be alive right now.

She could run to him, but there was too much space between this building and the woods.

Instead, she remained in place. She watched as, a moment later, a black SUV pulled up to the burned house.

That wasn't the police or firefighters.

That was the SUV the gunmen had been driving outside the café.

Two men climbed from the vehicle, guns drawn.

Men Emily had never seen before.

Had those men followed her here? Had they been hired by Conrad?

It made sense.

Despite their sunglasses that blocked their eyes, it was clear by the swivel of their heads that they were looking for someone.

Looking for *her*.

She remained where she was, hardly able to breathe.

The taller man, the one who'd been in the driver's seat, nodded toward the other man in silent conversation. Then they split up, each taking an opposite direction as they walked around the charred remains of her old house.

Her throat swelled as she waited.

What if they came this way? If they found her? Would they kill her on the spot?

Were these men the ones responsible for the fire? For taking Bree?

When they hadn't killed Emily the first time, had they come back now to do the job?

The questions pummeled her until her limbs shook and ice formed in her veins.

The men continued to circle her old house. Were they looking for her? Looking for something in the remains?

She wasn't sure. She wasn't sure about anything, really. Only that these guys were dangerous.

The barn was the closest structure. They would come here next.

Emily looked toward the trees again, toward where Austin hid.

She didn't know if she could make it there without being seen.

For now, she would wait. Her muscles were poised to act. Her mind raced. Her adrenaline pumped.

Emily looked back toward the men.

Sucked in a breath.

Only one man came into view. Where had the other gone?

There was a chance he'd walked to the other side of the barn when she hadn't been watching. A chance that he could be headed toward her now.

Just as the thought crossed her mind, a hand pressed hard over her mouth. Another one clamped her arms in place.

Panic raced through her as she prepared herself for whatever would happen next.

———

AUSTIN DIDN'T WANT to scare Emily, but he couldn't risk her making a sound.

He leaned in close, his lips practically brushing her ear. "It's me. I didn't want to frighten you, but you've got to stay quiet."

Her muscles loosened. As they did, he dropped his hands from around her and stepped back—though barely.

"If we stay here, they're going to find us," he continued. "You're going to have to come with me. I need you to trust me."

Emily looked up at him, a flash of doubt crossing her gaze. Despite that, she nodded. She'd always been reasonable.

He took her hand and led her around the barn, away from the men. They reached a window, and Austin boosted her through it. She climbed inside and landed in a stall on the other side.

Austin followed.

They paused, and Austin glanced around.

He knew he could fight those guys and take them down. But they were both armed, and he didn't want to put Emily in the line of fire.

Besides, while the men had been distracted, he'd put a tracking device on their vehicle. He needed them alive if they were going to lead him back to Bree.

"This way." He nodded at a wooden ladder leading to the hayloft.

"Are you sure that's safe?" Emily asked. "Joseph told me this barn was condemned. I was always afraid Bree would try to explore it."

Austin rattled the ladder. Stepped onto the first rung. Bounced. Then nodded.

"We have to be careful," he told her. "But we should be okay."

After a moment of hesitation, Emily began to climb slowly and carefully.

Austin followed behind.

At the top, he pointed to some bales of hay. "Back there."

As Austin pulled the ladder up into the loft, Emily scrambled in that direction.

Before she reached the hay bales, a noise sounded in the background.

The men.

They were coming into the barn.

She wasn't hidden yet.

Emily began to crawl faster.

The wood beneath her groaned.

Then splintered.

Then . . . it broke.

six

EMILY'S HEART felt like it might pound out of her chest as pieces of splintered wood and hay dropped to the floor below.

Her knee had gone through the floorboards.

Joseph had been right: this barn wasn't safe. This hayloft was just high enough to be dangerous. Maybe deadly.

Austin crouched beside her, not even a hint of anxiety on his calm features. It was like he did this every day. Maybe he did.

"It's okay," he murmured. "Keep going."

Voices drifted toward them.

Those men would see them any second.

Emily lifted her leg from the broken floorboard.

As she continued to crawl, her knee stung—but it

was nothing unbearable. She'd probably just scraped her skin.

Still, each movement was marred with hesitancy and caution.

Next time the wood broke . . . it might be more than her knee that fell through.

She prayed that wouldn't be the case.

Finally, she and Austin reached the bales and ducked behind them. Austin stayed close—almost too close.

Close enough that Emily could smell his cologne. At once, the familiar scent swept her back in time.

Back to when she'd relished the feeling of being in his arms. When she'd been intrigued by the man. When she'd been feeling rebellious.

What a mistake.

Her thoughts were cut short when the men came into view.

She froze and peered at them from a narrow opening between the bales.

Would they come up here and search for them? What if those men found them? Would Austin shoot them?

She had no idea.

So she waited. Tried to trust Austin.

However, it was hard to trust a man who hadn't

even given her his last name. Who'd lied about so many things. Who'd completely disappeared from her life, almost like he'd never even existed.

"Are you sure they came this way?" the taller of the two men asked.

"I've been tracking her phone." The shorter man stopped and glanced at his own cell phone. "It says she's been here."

These guys had tracked her phone? How had they been able to do that?

She'd led them right to her, and she'd been clueless.

She needed to get rid of it ASAP.

"How accurate are those readings?" Tall Man asked.

"You know how these things are. The tracker doesn't narrow a location down to the exact area. She could be anywhere around here."

"Or maybe your app just isn't updating," Tall Guy said. "I don't see any signs she's been here."

Emily's heart thumped in her ears.

Good. Maybe they would leave.

But she wouldn't relax. Not yet.

Not until she knew these guys were gone.

———

AUSTIN KEPT his hand on Emily's arm, reminding her not to make any sudden moves.

She remained frozen.

He could grab his gun and be ready to shoot in zero-point-six seconds. Literally. He'd been timed. But he had to remain on guard.

"Boss isn't going to be happy," Tall Man said. "The job seemed so simple."

"Nothing's ever simple." The other guy wandered around the barn, looking behind stall doors, gun still in hand.

"I don't even understand this assignment."

"It's not ours to understand. We just do what we're told."

Tall Guy grunted and kept looking.

These guys weren't top-shelf hired hands. Not at all.

The fact that they were talking right now indicated they weren't that experienced. Anyone who knew what they were doing would know to be quiet. Would know the element of surprise was important.

But Austin hoped to use that to his advantage. Maybe these guys would say something to indicate where Bree was or who was behind this.

At least their mistakes might benefit Austin.

No way these guys would be sneaking up on them.

It was a wonder the police hadn't followed them here. Certainly, law enforcement was all over the scene of the shooting back in Lancaster. Finding these men would be at the top of their priority list.

Then the men paused. Glanced at the hayloft.

"Should we check up there?" the tall guy asked.

Austin's gut clenched as he waited to see what the men would do next.

seven

EMILY COULDN'T BREATHE. She didn't want to think about what might happen next.

She imagined the men finding them. A gun battle. An uncertain outcome.

Then Tall Guy shook his head, still staring at his colleague's phone. "She's not here. I don't know what happened with this tracker on her phone."

"Maybe it's a glitch."

A moment later, the men left the barn.

Emily released her breath. That had felt close. Too close.

She didn't dare speak or move until she heard their SUV pulling away a few minutes later.

"You okay?" Austin asked.

She nodded.

"Good job staying still."

She felt as if she should say thank you, but she only nodded instead.

Austin shifted, and the wood creaked beneath him, a reminder of the precarious situation they were in right now. One wrong move, and they could fall to their death. This wood was so old and brittle that she could feel it warping beneath her weight. Various other holes and cracks proved this wasn't the first time someone had been up here and in danger.

"Let's slowly crawl to the ladder." A serious look stained his gaze. "I'll let you go down first. But you need to be careful, okay?"

"Of course." But Emily's legs trembled with every movement as she started toward the edge of the hayloft.

As they reached the ladder, Austin carefully lowered it back to the floor.

She hesitated before shifting in order to climb down.

The loft creaked beneath her again before a soft, splintering sound filled the air.

Her throat tightened.

Not again . . .

Wasting no more time, she situated herself and

started down. Austin remained above her, holding the top of the ladder in place.

Finally, she reached the bottom. Wiped the hay from her clothes and hair. Then she held the ladder for Austin.

He skipped the last several rungs and jumped down, landing with a thud on his feet.

Her throat went dry when she realized just how fit he was. She didn't want to be impressed, but Austin *was* impressive. He was strong with defined muscles and sure motions. He always seemed calm, like he knew exactly what he was doing. His mind always seemed to be calculating his next move.

She averted her gaze so he wouldn't see her staring.

Not missing a beat, he held out his hand. "Let me have your phone."

She handed it to him, wondering what he would do.

To her horror, he walked outside and tossed it into the field.

She hurried behind him. "Why did you do that?"

"Those men are tracking you using your phone."

Panic surged in her until she could hardly breathe. "What if the kidnapper calls? I need to know what their demands are. I need to do what they say if I'm going to get Bree back."

"They probably won't give you demands, Emily."

Her eyes widened as she tried to process what he said. "Why wouldn't they give me any demands?"

He cocked his head, but his voice remained soft. "Have they given you any demands yet?"

The truth of what he was saying bore down on her, though she didn't want to acknowledge it. "Only not to tell the police."

"They have no interest in giving her back. They want to keep her." He shrugged. "I'm sorry, Emily. But that's the truth."

Emily wanted to deny his statement. But Austin was probably right. The kidnapper had made no offers that would allow Emily to get her daughter back. They'd only tried to kill Emily.

Her head spun at the thought, and she wobbled.

Austin gripped her elbow to steady her.

"I'm sorry." His voice softened. "I shouldn't have been so blunt."

She wanted to tell him it was okay, that she didn't want him to soften the truth. She needed to know the reality of the situation, no matter how painful it was. But the words wouldn't leave her lips.

Instead, she stared at Austin another moment.

Who exactly was this man? He'd told her that he

was in the military. But that had been a lie. One of many that he'd told her.

She'd done her research. Had talked to the owner of the bar where they'd met. Had gotten an image of Austin from the security video. She'd showed the image to base commanders at all the local military bases, and no one recognized him.

Lies . . . everything he'd told her had been lies.

She clamped her mouth shut. She had no room to talk. Truthfully, she was withholding certain details from him also, so she needed to be careful not to be too self-righteous.

But if he only knew . . .

Soon, she'd have to tell him about what had happened after their little fling together. She couldn't put off sharing the truth much longer.

But now didn't seem like the right time. They needed to be free of distractions. Plus, the stress of that conversation was enough to put her over the edge.

She wasn't sure how much more she could handle right now.

Because her whole world had already been turned upside down.

————

AUSTIN LED EMILY BACK to his car. He'd seen enough here.

He cranked his engine and backed out of the woods where he'd stashed his vehicle.

He felt Emily's gaze on him as he started down the lane, felt the unspoken questions.

"Why do you look like you know where you're going right now?" she finally asked.

"Because I do."

She crossed her arms. "Would you care to fill me in?"

"I put a tracker on that SUV," he explained. "I want to see where those guys are going."

He couldn't be sure, but Emily might have looked impressed as her eyebrows flickered up.

But he didn't care about impressing her right now. He needed to get her daughter back. Do the job. Move on to his next assignment.

There wouldn't be any rekindling of feelings from the past. Not that Emily would be interested in more. They'd gone into things with no strings attached.

He wasn't normally a hit-and-run relationship kind of guy. At least he hadn't been in recent years.

Not since Emily, actually. His time with her had changed him. Afterward, he'd hit rock bottom, and he'd vowed to never go back to that way of living again.

His changes had been real, and he hadn't looked back. But those lessons had come at a high cost.

Not that Emily would ever believe that.

Focus, Austin. Focus.

A dot appeared on the screen on his dash.

"Is that indicating where the SUV is going?" Emily asked.

"Yes, it is."

Austin followed the trail as he drove through the back roads of Amish country.

Twenty minutes later, they came upon an older, historic-looking neighborhood that had seen better days. The houses had once been beautiful with colorful siding and wide front porches. Though a few homes had been restored, most looked like they could use a fresh coat of paint or a good power wash.

He stopped a few houses down and pointed. "That's where they are."

Emily stared at the place, her body trembling.

The two-story house with its purple siding and neat but simple flowerbeds looked ordinary and unassuming.

Was this where Bree was being held?

He needed to find out.

eight

EMILY STARED at the house only a second before reaching for her door.

If Bree was inside, she needed to find her.

Before she could tug the handle, Austin's hand covered her shoulder. "You can't."

She swerved her head until her gaze met his. "If my daughter's in there then we need to get her. There's no time to waste."

Austin shook his head, compassion filling his gaze. "It's too dangerous. You don't want to put her in a position where she could be harmed."

His words stopped her cold, and she froze. No, she couldn't put her daughter in danger. Handling this in the wrong way could do that.

"I can't just sit here," Emily murmured, hating the helpless feeling that washed over her again.

"That's exactly what I need you to do." His voice sounded stern and authoritative. "I'm going to get a closer look, but I need you to stay here."

"But—"

"You can't go." His gaze bore into hers. "You have to promise me you won't try. I can't have you risking this whole operation. I know you think you know what you're doing, but you don't. I'm trained for these kinds of situations. I don't have the same emotional component as you since Bree isn't my child."

She stared at him. Licked her lips. Contemplated what to say.

Because the truth was . . . Bree was his child.

Only he didn't know it.

Because Emily had never known his last name. She'd tried to track him down through the military. She'd had no luck.

She'd gone back to the bar where they'd met. No one knew his full name.

The bartender promised to call her if he came back in. She'd never heard anything.

She'd hit dead end after dead end.

Finally, she'd stopped trying.

Was this the time to tell him the truth?

The timing didn't seem right.

Was there ever a good time, though?

Emily opened her mouth, unsure what to say.

Before any words could leave her lips, Austin dipped his head lower until they were eye to eye. "You promise you'll stay here?"

He waited for her to respond.

Knowing there was no more time to waste, Emily nodded. "I promise."

Austin slipped out and put the top to the convertible up—not that the canvas would offer much protection. But she felt safer and less exposed, at least.

As he walked away, Emily began praying again . . . praying they could find her—their—daughter and that Bree would remain safe.

No prayer she'd ever murmured had been as desperate.

———

WHY HAD Emily looked like she had more to say? Austin wondered. Almost as if she was about to share some type of revelation? Were his suspicions correct, and was there something important she wasn't telling him?

It didn't matter right now.

He needed to focus.

He tried to erase the haunted look in her eyes from his mind as he crept toward the house.

He assumed those two guys he'd seen at Emily's old place were inside.

What he really wanted was to see if Bree was inside also. He knew it was a long shot. That most likely he wouldn't be able to peer inside any windows and spot the girl there.

But maybe he could see signs of her having been there.

Making sure no one else was watching, he skulked around the building.

A window was cracked open a few inches, and he glanced inside.

Those two guys sat at a kitchen table drinking beer. They were taking a load off as they shot the breeze, most likely waiting for other instructions from "Boss."

He scanned the kitchen as they talked, but he didn't see any kid friendly snacks. No toys. No clothing.

Nothing that indicated Bree had been here.

Austin stepped to the side and pressed his back to the wall so he could listen without being spotted.

"What's our next move?" Tall Guy said.

"No idea. I'm just waiting for instructions."

"You think the police are onto us yet?"

"Doubt it, especially not since I changed the plates."

"Smart thinking. We just gotta stay one step ahead of them."

"Whatever makes the boss happy."

A stick cracked behind him, and Austin froze.

Had he been discovered?

nine

EMILY RUBBED HER THROAT, feeling as if she couldn't breathe.

She could no longer see Austin.

Was he still creeping around the house? Had he seen anything inside? What if those guys found him? What would she do then?

The questions pummeled her, and she reminded herself not to worry.

Helping people deal with various issues was what she did for a living. At least, it was what she *had* done for a living. She'd talked people through their problems. Taught them how to overcome things like anxiety, depression, and grief.

Right now, she couldn't seem to take any of her own advice. Her thoughts barreled out of control. Her breathing exercises didn't work. Her prayers felt unanswered.

Her blood rushed through her ears, and a sheen of moisture covered her forehead.

Her daughter had been kidnapped. There was no way she wouldn't have anxiety in a situation like this.

Although she assumed Paul's family had taken Bree, it was only an assumption.

She'd tried to call Conrad last night and then again this morning.

He hadn't answered.

That fact seemed to confirm her suspicions that he was behind this.

Emily had even talked to his secretary, who'd made up some flimsy excuse before muttering that he would be returning tomorrow.

Maybe part of her hoped Conrad was behind this. Because Conrad kidnapping Bree was better than a stranger doing so.

He wouldn't hurt Bree.

But if it wasn't Conrad. Then who? Why?

Her mind produced horrific possibilities.

Someone who'd taken her because they were unable to have a child of their own. Someone who took her because they were lonely.

Or . . . what if Bree was being sold into human trafficking?

A cry left Emily's lips before she could stop it. She slapped a hand over her mouth—not that there was anyone around to hear her.

She hadn't gotten any more correspondence. No more texts or demands from the abductor.

Now she didn't have a phone.

What if Austin was right? What if the kidnappers didn't plan on sending her any demands because they had no intention of returning Bree?

Her throat burned as emotion welled within her, nearly sending her panic into a tailspin.

Finally, Austin appeared on the sidewalk, looking at ease as if he were taking a casual walk. Emily couldn't read his expression or body language as he headed toward the car.

As soon as he climbed back into the Mustang and slammed the door, she rushed, "Well?"

She knew she sounded impatient, but she didn't apologize for it. Her mental timer was going strong, and she knew minutes were ticking away entirely too quickly. With every second, the chances she would get Bree back diminished.

She could hardly stomach the thought.

Austin turned toward her and ran a hand through

his hair. "I didn't see any signs Bree had been there. There was one room I couldn't see inside of. But listening to the guys, I don't think they're holding her there."

"But she *could* be there." Emily's pitch lilted higher.

She'd been so hopeful that Bree would be inside. That Austin would see her. That this nightmare might end.

"We can't just leave," Emily continued. "What if there's a basement?"

"I called some of my colleagues, and they're going to give me a hand. As soon as these guys leave, my guys will go inside and see if she was there." Austin paused and studied her a moment. "We're going to find her, Emily. We will. But it might take some time."

A tear escaped and slowly made its way down Emily's cheek.

She wanted to believe Austin. She really did.

But he'd let her down before.

What if he let her down now also?

———

AUSTIN'S THROAT tightened as he sat in the car and watched the tears pour down Emily's face.

More than anything, he wanted to reach for her. To offer her some comfort.

But he knew his touch wouldn't be welcome.

Instead, he sat there helplessly.

Maybe sitting quietly was the best thing to do anyway. He'd been trained in all things tactical. In warfare. In special operations and code-breaking and forensics.

But reading women?

Most definitely not.

He gave Emily a moment.

As he did, he kept an eye on everything around them. He needed to remain on guard, just in case.

Thankfully, the sound he'd heard outside the house had just been a squirrel. The animal had quickly scampered away when it saw Austin there.

But the more he learned about Bree's disappearance, the more tension grew inside him.

He needed to talk to Larchmont.

It couldn't be a coincidence that he and Emily had been pushed back together like this.

He didn't believe in fate.

But he *did* believe in God's divine providence. Maybe God had brought them back together for a reason.

He had to believe that everything happened for a purpose.

Even everything with Brigitta and Carlos, two of his most challenging assignments.

He'd tried to leave those cases in his past, but he was fooling himself.

The past was a part of his present and his future.

"What do we do now?" Emily sniffled and drew in a shaky breath as if trying to pull herself together.

"We wait," he told her. "We see if these guys leave. Where they go. Being patient is important. Backup will be here soon. Until then, we don't let these guys out of our sight."

ten

EMILY STRAIGHTENED AND grabbed Austin's arm. "Look. They're leaving!"

Austin sat up straighter but remained quiet.

"What should we do? Should we look inside the house ourselves? Or should we follow them?" She glanced at Austin, waiting for his reply.

"I don't think Bree is in there." Austin's jaw tightened. "But I'd like to have my friends check it out. They were in Philly and should be here soon. For now, I think our best bet is to follow these guys."

Emily opened her mouth, wanting to argue. But she had to trust him. Austin knew what he was doing in this situation, and she didn't. Trusting others with the wellbeing of her child was difficult, but she had to be logical here.

"Okay," she finally said. "If that's what you think is best."

As the SUV pulled away, Austin waited a moment before following them.

Austin's vehicle of choice was conspicuous, to say the least. But maybe he hadn't anticipated this. If he was as skilled as she'd been told, then this had clearly been an oversight.

Besides, she vaguely remembered talking to him when they'd first met, and he'd mentioned something about his love for fast cars.

Austin expertly maneuvered into traffic, keeping a comfortable distance behind the SUV. He seemed to know a lot about a lot. Seemed to be an expert in many areas—tactical, investigative, defensive.

She'd known military guys before. None of them would know how to handle themselves in this kind of situation like Austin did. He seemed to have special training and phenomenal instincts.

Maybe Austin had been CIA. Was that possible? Was saying he was military just a cover story?

For years she'd tried to figure out where Austin had gone and how she could find him. Then she'd settled on the fact she was trying for the impossible. Austin was practically a ghost. Bree would never know her real father.

But now that Emily had run into Austin again, she wondered if maybe it was best Bree didn't know.

Austin was gruff. Could be rough around the edges. His gaze had a certain shadow to it.

Was this the kind of man she wanted in her daughter's life? Someone so dangerous and mysterious? Someone more comfortable with holding a gun than helping with a homework assignment?

But not speaking the truth wouldn't be fair to Austin or Bree.

She had to tell Austin about Bree, especially now that their paths had collided again.

Besides, something seemed different about him now.

When they first met, she'd been swept away by his larger-than-life personality.

She'd been in a stage where she'd made some very bad choices.

For one night, she wanted to see how the other half lived. She'd always tried to be a good girl, and it had gotten her nowhere. Why bother following the rules if the rules only left you with heartache?

Her fiancé had left her. She didn't get into her first-choice doctorate program. Her parents had announced they were divorcing after thirty years of marriage.

She'd wanted to throw caution to the wind.

So she did.

As Austin made a sharp turn in the Mustang, the motion jerked Emily from her thoughts. She'd have to ponder those questions more later. Ponder the best way to even bring up the subject.

The SUV turned into the parking lot of a burger joint.

A restaurant? How could those guys stop to eat in the middle of all this?

Austin pulled off the road and into an adjoining lot.

What would his next plan of action be?

———

AUSTIN LET OUT A LONG BREATH.

In different circumstances—if those men hadn't seen his face outside the café—he'd suggest he should go inside the restaurant and eavesdrop.

But Austin couldn't do that. His presence would be too obvious.

He would be spotted right away if he went inside.

Instead, he watched as the two men climbed out and headed into a burger joint.

How could they look so casual? Especially if they'd just kidnapped a child?

Except Austin wasn't 100 percent sure those two had kidnapped anyone.

He felt as if he was missing something. Like there was some other important detail Emily was hiding. He just wasn't sure what.

He needed more time to talk with her so he could get to the bottom of this.

"Should we go back to the house? Check it out while they eat?" Emily's voice cut into his thoughts.

Just as she asked the question, his phone buzzed.

It was a text from Gage Pearson, one of his colleagues. He and another colleague, Trevor McGrath, had already arrived at the house. Thank goodness, they'd been close.

Which begged another question: if Gage and Trevor were so close, why hadn't Larchmont sent them instead of having Austin fly up from New Orleans to take this assignment?

If there was one thing Austin knew about his boss, it was the fact the man didn't do anything without good reason.

He'd think about that more later.

For now, Austin read the message and shared it with Emily.

"Should we meet them there?" she rushed.

"Let them do their job. Believe me, if they find your daughter, they won't leave her."

Emily stared at him, doubt still in her gaze.

"My colleagues and I are the best at what we do," Austin assured her. "I know it's hard to trust us, but I'm asking you to do that."

Questions still circled in her gaze, and he could understand why.

He had a lot he needed to explain. About who he was. About that night they'd met.

But not now. Not yet.

"We're going to have to find somewhere for you to stay tonight," Austin finally said. "Somewhere these guys can't find you."

Emily nodded silently.

Austin studied her another moment, realizing how gaunt she looked. "When was the last time you ate?"

She shrugged. "I don't know."

"You don't remember?"

She shrugged again. "It's been an extremely stressful twenty-four hours."

That was answer enough. Emily hadn't eaten since Bree disappeared.

He knew Emily didn't want to be distracted from looking for Bree. But she would need help herself if she didn't get some food into her system.

He needed to convince her to eat—and they could talk more as they did. They certainly still had a lot of conversations that needed to be had.

eleven

EMILY WATCHED as Austin pulled to a stop in front of an Amish restaurant they'd passed a couple of miles up the road.

"The woman seated beside me on the flight here told me all about it," Austin explained. "She convinced me it was worth giving a try. You ever eaten here before?"

Emily shook her head. "No, but I've heard about it. Heard the food is good."

"Let's see if we can get a table. You need to eat, and we need to talk. This looks like a good place to do so." He paused. "It will be my treat."

"Thank you. I'll pay you back as soon as I have access to my money."

Thankfully, they'd missed the dinner rush.

Austin requested a corner table, no doubt because he wanted to see everyone who came and went. The waitress accommodated them.

The restaurant wasn't fancy with its wood panel walls, outdated floors, and mismatched tables. However, the smells were amazing.

Yeasty bread. Roasted meat. Sweet, doughy pies.

Emily couldn't wait to try something.

They sat down, and a basket of biscuits and corn-bread was placed in front of them. They both ordered specials off the menu: chicken and dumplings for Emily, and pot roast, mashed potatoes, and green beans for Austin.

Then a moment of silence fell.

Emily munched on an airy biscuit, trying to think of small talk—something she despised.

Finally, she asked, "So . . . when did you get out of the military?"

"Three years ago." Austin took a long sip of his sweet tea.

"And you began working for the Shadow Agency?"

He nodded, his gaze guarded. "That's right. My former commander left the military about the same time and decided to start the Shadow Agency. He recruited me and some of my friends to be a part of it."

"I see. And how do you like it?" Emily tried to be careful how she worded her questions. She didn't want to sound like a therapist trying to get information from him. It was a hazard of the job, she supposed.

"I like it," he said. "It fits my lifestyle."

His lifestyle? Was he still a nomad? Someone who didn't want to settle down?

Most likely.

He'd been all wrong for her—and he still was.

Not that Emily was hoping for anything more. Not by any means.

She never wanted to have a man in her life again. Her life was better with just her and Bree. Marrying Paul had been a mistake—one she didn't want to make twice.

As soon as their orders came, Austin's phone rang, and he answered. Emily couldn't tell what the conversation was about, though she was curious.

He ended the call and turned back to her. "My colleagues were able to get into the house."

"And?"

"There were no signs of Bree there. Of any child being there, for that matter. They checked the attic and looked for any hidden rooms even. The place is clear."

Emily's shoulders sank with disappointment. "I see."

"They're going to the burger joint where the men are to see if they can overhear anything. Then they're going to tail these guys and see if the guys lead them anywhere. I have a feeling those two won't leave town, though."

She studied his face. "Why do you say that?"

"I think these guys were hired to do this job. They won't leave until they've . . . finished."

A shiver raked through her. "You mean until I'm dead?"

Compassion flickered in his gaze, and he softened his voice. "To be blunt, yes. But I'm not sure if they're the ones who actually kidnapped Bree. Either way, they're hired hands. They're not the masterminds."

Emily could see where he was coming from. Neither of those men looked like the type who would call the shots. They were simply following orders.

Orders from Conrad?

Maybe.

She closed her eyes and lifted a silent prayer for her food. When she opened her eyes again, Austin had a strange look in his gaze as he watched her.

Then he looked away, not saying anything.

Did he think it was strange that she prayed? Especially considering her past?

Maybe.

She set that thought aside and took a bite of the chicken and dumplings. They were surprisingly tasty —but just bland enough to help settle her stomach.

As she took another bite, another thought hit her.

This seemed like the perfect opportunity to tell Austin the truth. But Emily wasn't even sure how to bring it up. The subject wasn't to be taken lightly, not something to be said in casual conversation.

Anxiety churned inside her.

Emily took another bite of her dinner and tried to build up her courage.

AUSTIN TRIED NOT to stare at Emily from across the table.

But he couldn't seem to stop himself from stealing glances.

When he'd seen her for the first time seven years ago, he'd been blown away. He thought he'd never seen someone so beautiful. So out of his league.

She'd been sitting alone at a bar when he

approached. She hadn't even seemed that interested in talking to him. Instead, she looked deep in thought.

But after several minutes, the conversation was flowing as easily as the alcohol, especially when they both discovered they liked country music. Not the new country music. But the old stuff. Vince Gill. Randy Travis. Alan Jackson.

Austin had felt on top of the world. Not only was Emily pretty, but she was smart and funny. Not the type of woman he expected to see in a place like that.

He'd been in Norfolk, Virginia, at a dive bar frequented by sailors who needed to blow off steam between deployments.

Austin had been going there more than he should have, mostly because he'd been wrestling with his future.

The experiments he was undergoing as part of Project Elevate were beginning to get to him. But he'd felt as if he were in too deep, like he couldn't back out.

Yet that was all he'd wanted to do.

If he could go back and change things . . .

But what other options had he had? His dad had kicked him out. His mom was dead. His older brother had it worse than Austin did. He'd been in jail at that point.

Austin's future hadn't seemed hopeful. When he'd

been offered the chance to get involved with Project Elevate, he'd thought it seemed like a golden opportunity.

He'd been wrong. So, so wrong.

"Austin?"

Emily's voice pulled him from his heavy thoughts, and he snapped back to the present. If she'd been talking, he hadn't heard a word.

"Are you okay?" A wrinkle formed on her brow as she studied him.

He ate the last bite of his pot roast and waved her off. "I'm fine. Just thinking."

He wouldn't dare tell her what he'd been thinking about.

She stared at him as if unconvinced. But she nodded anyway.

This was a bad idea, he realized. He shouldn't be working this case. Since Gage and Trevor were in town, he should give the investigation to one of them. It made more sense.

He and Emily had a past, and their history might get in the way. Their prior relationship might cloud his judgment.

Why had Larchmont given him this assignment?

Austin would be sure to ask him next time they spoke.

For now, he and Emily were going to order dessert. Then he'd find a motel for the night. Once Emily was settled there, he'd give Larchmont a call and gracefully back out of this assignment.

Because one thing was sure.

Emily had been too good for him then, and she was still too good for him now.

twelve

EMILY HAD STARTED to tell Austin about Bree.

Her throat had gone bone dry. Her voice had sounded crackly. She'd licked her lips one too many times.

But as she'd attempted to start, she realized Austin wasn't listening. His mind seemed to be in another world as he stared out a nearby window.

It seemed a sign that this wasn't a good time.

There was so much she didn't know about him. But she was still curious today, just as she'd been curious seven years ago. What was going on behind those brooding eyes of his? What had led him to this point in life? Why did he have those scars on his arms and back?

It didn't matter. It wasn't her business. The more distance she could keep, the better.

She'd be wise to remember that.

As soon as they finished dessert, Austin stood and dropped some cash on the table before nodding toward the door. "We should go."

"Why the rush? Did something happen?" Had one of his colleagues texted with an update?

"It's better if you get somewhere out of the public eye. Just to be on the safe side."

After settling into the car and starting down the road, Austin chatted on the phone as he drove, using his AirPods to hear the other end of the conversation. Emily tried to interpret what was being said, but it was no use.

He'd tell her anything important . . . hopefully.

She noticed that Austin kept an eye on the rearview mirror as he drove. He was still on guard. That made her feel both better and worse.

Finally, they reached the motel. Austin got them a room and began to usher her upstairs.

"This will be a good place to lie low for now," Austin said. "You can't risk going back to the hotel the relief organization reserved for you."

"I agree."

They paused by the door, and Austin hesitated.

She sensed something else was going on.

"Listen," Austin started. "Trevor is going to take over for me."

Her heart leapt into her throat. "What? Why?"

"Considering the history between you and me, I don't think it's a good idea that I'm lead on this assignment. But Trevor will do a great job and help you get your daughter back. I'm leaving you in good hands."

Emily grabbed his arm. "But I don't want Trevor. I want you."

Austin stared at her, questions in his gaze. Then, as quickly as they appeared, they disappeared.

He stepped back, and Emily's arm dropped down beside her. "I think it's for the best. I'll get you settled, then I'll be on my way. Trevor is almost here, and I need to talk to him."

As Austin started to step away, panic gripped her. If Emily let him walk away now, she might not ever be able to track him down again. She couldn't miss the opportunity.

She grabbed his arm again, desperate to get through to him somehow.

Austin turned back toward her, a knot of confusion between his eyes.

"Please, Austin." Her voice trembled. "I need it to

be you. You asked me to trust you. Now I'm asking you to trust me."

His knot of confusion only grew deeper. "Why would you need me specifically? I know we have some history. But, in truth, we hardly know each other."

Emily licked her lips and rubbed her hands on her jeans. "Austin . . . I've been trying to gather up the courage to tell you this, and I didn't know how."

"Just spit it out then."

She swallowed hard. "It's about Bree."

"What about her?"

"She's . . ." Emily swallowed hard again. "She's your daughter."

———

EMILY'S WORDS echoed in Austin's ears.

Certainly, he hadn't heard her correctly. There was no way what she'd said was true.

Bree wasn't his daughter.

She couldn't be.

Yet, he knew she could.

A niggle of truth begged for his attention.

When he'd seen a picture of Bree, he'd seen similarities to himself. But he hadn't thought much of it. Coincidence, he'd assumed.

Because the idea was absurd.

And it was *still* absurd.

If he had a child, he would have known . . . right?

He turned back to Emily and saw the tight lines on her face. "I don't know what kind of game you're playing . . ."

"I'm not playing a game." She pressed her lips together and swallowed. "I promise."

"We were only together that one night." He stared at her, trying to grasp onto the truth.

He knew Trevor was waiting in the lot for him. That didn't matter right now.

He had to finish this conversation. He had to know more.

"I can explain." The sides of Emily's eyes were crinkled with worry and her lips pulled down in a frown. "I just need a few minutes of your time. No one wants to find Bree as much as I do. And maybe her dad. Her *real* dad. That's why I need you to do this job. Please."

Austin raked a hand through his hair, his head still spinning. His thoughts didn't know where to go. This was all too much.

Could she be telling the truth? Why would she lie about this?

He couldn't think of a single reason why she would.

"You and I need to talk." He leveled his gaze with her, and his voice dropped at least an octave deeper. "To really talk."

"I agree." Emily nodded quickly.

"I'm going to get you inside. Then I need to talk to Trevor. After that I'll be back to finish this conversation."

She nodded quickly again.

Austin unlocked the door to their second-floor room. He checked the place out before instructing Emily to stay there.

Then he slipped outside to talk to his colleague. He knew, however, that he'd have a hard time concentrating on anything other than the bombshell Emily had just dropped.

Could he really be a father?

If it turned out to be true . . .

That sounded like a total disaster.

thirteen

AUSTIN MET TREVOR OUTSIDE.

Trevor was in his early thirties, tall, blond, and muscular. The two of them had worked together on many assignments in the past, and Austin knew he was a stand-up guy.

Trevor told Austin he hadn't seen or heard anything suspicious when he followed those men. Gage was still watching them.

Austin didn't mention anything about what Emily had told him—and he had no intention of bringing it up.

Not now. Maybe not ever.

He had to make sense of things first.

When they finished talking, Trevor handed Austin

some bags of clothing and toiletries he'd picked up for Emily as well as Austin's duffel bag.

Then the two traded vehicles.

Gage would keep an eye on those men while Trevor stayed in the area overnight in case Austin needed anything.

Austin felt better knowing backup was close. The guys after Emily were more aggressive than he'd assumed they'd be.

He walked back up to the room.

Dread settled between his shoulders, pinching each of his muscles. The pressure became tighter and tighter the closer he got to the room.

How would Emily explain this one? Was she making this whole story up so he'd stay on the case?

But what sense would that make? Why would she want him on the case instead of someone else?

The truth was . . . she had no reason to lie. Not as far as he knew.

He used his key to unlock the door and stepped inside.

The motel was slightly rundown with outdated furnishings. But it appeared clean, other than the odor inside.

What was that? Dust? Mold? Pungent cleaners? Maybe a mix of all three.

As soon as he saw Emily sitting on the edge of the bed with her distraught gaze, he knew this wasn't a ploy to get him to stay. Her turmoil was real.

He sank onto the edge of the bed across from Emily and studied her. Saw her red eyes. Her shaky motions.

"I'm ready," he finally said.

But was he really? Was anyone really ready for that kind of news?

Emily licked her lips.

But before she could start, shouts sounded from the outside walkway.

Tension embedded itself between Austin's shoulders as he strode toward the window.

EMILY HELD HER BREATH.

Had more trouble found them?

Her heart felt as if it might pound out of her chest.

Austin raced toward the window and peered outside. He didn't say anything, but his body remained stiff.

"Austin?" Her voice sounded scratchy as she said his name.

"It's just a couple having some type of argument," he muttered. "They just went into their room."

"So this doesn't pertain to us?"

He dropped the curtain. "No, it doesn't."

Relief swept through her. But the emotion was short-lived as Austin turned toward her.

"But it does sound like there are other very important matters that do pertain to us." He didn't bother to hide the curiosity—and maybe even the touch of concern—in his voice.

As he sat back on the bed opposite her, Emily thought she might be sick to her stomach. But she'd already opened Pandora's box, as the saying went. Now she had to explain everything to him.

She rubbed her neck, which suddenly ached. "About three months after you and I were . . . were . . . *together*, I realized I hadn't been feeling well. On a whim, I took a pregnancy test." She swallowed hard. "It was positive."

He narrowed his eyes. "How do you know it was me?"

She gave him a look. "Because I wasn't lying to you when I told you I wasn't the type of girl to have one-night stands. For a high achiever, I wasn't handling life's disappointments very well then. So I decided to cut loose for a night. I wish I could say it was a mistake

. . . in many ways, I suppose it was. But then there was Bree . . .”

“So you’re saying you weren’t with anyone else?” He continued to study her as if searching for the truth.

She looked him in the eye and nodded. “That’s correct. Only you.”

“But . . .”

“I know you took measures to ensure it didn’t happen. But those measures didn’t work.”

Realization rolled over his features. “Okay . . . and why didn’t you try to find me?”

His words ignited something inside her, frustration she’d pent up for years. She tried to keep the irritation from her voice, though she knew she wasn’t successful. “It wasn’t easy since all I knew was your first name. You didn’t give me a last name.”

“That was part of our deal, wasn’t it?”

“I went back to the club and asked around, but no one knew your last name,” she continued. “I got your picture from the security cameras there. I even went to all the nearby military bases looking for you. But they said there was no one there that fit your description.”

He blinked in surprise. “Really?”

“Really. At that point, short of putting out a newspaper ad—which still wouldn’t have been effective because you’d have to read the newspaper to see it—I didn't know what to do. So I just tried to make the best of things."

"I see." He ran a hand over his mouth, his gaze still filled with disbelief.

Emily studied him, wondering what he was thinking.

Then she gave him a moment to process everything she'd just said.

It was a lot to absorb. She knew it was.

But she hoped he believed her . . . because everything she said was true.

She could prove it with a DNA test. But that would take time, and time was something she didn't have.

fourteen

AUSTIN TRIED to make sense of Emily's words.

He wanted to deny them. To somehow blame her for this.

But he couldn't. Because what she'd said made sense.

Although . . . it did seem as if someone at one of the military bases could have IDed him somehow.

Except he'd needed to be nameless and faceless to do the jobs he'd done. For that reason, the military denied any association. If he'd been caught, the US would claim he didn't work for them.

Austin had been going through a hard time that night.

He'd wanted out of the program he'd been asked to be a part of. He was tired of feeling like a lab rat.

Unhappy with the realization that he could never have a real future. His career demanded everything from him, and relationships were frowned upon.

He'd been questioning his choices. His future. Some of his missions even.

He'd had an existential crisis, he supposed.

But, from the start, he'd been upfront with Emily. He'd told her he wasn't looking for anything serious.

She'd told him she understood. She'd said that she wasn't either. No strings attached.

His thoughts zoomed all over the place.

To the surprise over how Emily could have gotten pregnant.

To the shock that she insisted Bree had to be his.

To curiosity about how the rest of the story had played out.

Austin stared at her. "I assumed Paul was the father."

She let out a deep sigh. "When I was five months along, I met Paul at a coffee shop. I was studying for one of my classes when he asked if he could sit across from me. I said yes. We talked for the next two hours, and he asked me for my phone number."

"Takes a lot of guts to hit on a pregnant woman."

Emily shrugged. "He had a lot of 'guts' then. We

started to date and got married a month before Bree was born."

"Fast . . ."

"I suppose being pregnant sped things up a bit."

"How did Paul die?" Austin continued to try to put all the pieces together.

"He was in the wrong place at the wrong time, I guess you could say. That's the short version."

Austin ran a hand over his face again. He didn't know what to think about all this.

But if what Emily had told him was true . . . then he was a father.

A little girl's father.

He didn't have time to relish the idea or wonder how the news might change his life.

Because his daughter had been kidnapped.

And he was even more determined now to find her.

———

EMILY STARED AT AUSTIN, trying to read his expression.

She'd known when she met him in the bar that evening that he was a player.

He wasn't her type at all. She always dated serious,

intellectual men who were business-minded and career-focused.

She wasn't even interested in military guys. That was why she'd gone to that bar sailors always frequented.

None of her actions that night had fit her personality.

The next morning, she'd been so disappointed in herself. She should have known better. She'd always been the good girl who played it safe and followed the rules.

That choice had changed the rest of her life.

But she'd never ever call Bree a mistake.

Emily swallowed hard and stood, suddenly unable to sit still. "I wish there was more I could tell you. But there's not."

Austin's expression looked weary, like he'd been handed a thousand burdens all at once. "You've got to understand that this is a lot for me to comprehend."

"Of course." She paused. "I *did* want you to know. I didn't care about money or child support so much. I just thought it was the right thing. Then when I couldn't track you down . . . I eventually had to move on. I was out of options, and I'd already wasted so much time."

"I get that. I . . . I still don't know what to say. Are

you telling me the fact the two of us met today is a coincidence?" He stared hard as if not wanting to miss any hint of deceit.

Emily let out a dry laugh. "I still can't believe it either."

Silence passed for a moment.

"Did Paul adopt Bree?" Austin's voice sounded raw as he asked the question.

"No . . . he talked about it, but he never did. My name is the only one on her birth certificate."

Austin nodded slowly, unreadable emotions hovering in his gaze.

He cleared his throat before asking, "How did you say you found the Shadow Agency? We don't advertise. We get our clients by word of mouth."

"Like I told you earlier, a man came up to me after the fire and handed me a business card. He said he'd be able to help, that I should give him a call. At that point, I figured I didn't have anything to lose."

"Can you describe this man?"

"He was tall and fairly thin with salt-and-pepper hair."

Austin nodded slowly as if trying to comprehend that.

"Does he sound familiar to you?" Emily wanted

more information. Wanted to put the pieces together. Wanted answers to *something*.

"He *might* match the description of my boss, Larchmont. Although, I don't know why Larchmont would intentionally do this. But believe me, I *will* be having a talk with him."

"As you should."

"As a matter of fact, I think I'm going to do that right now. I need some answers. If my boss knew I had a daughter and didn't tell me . . ." Austin stood, his hands clenched at his side.

"But . . . how could he possibly know? I mean, I looked for you for several weeks. But I didn't tell anyone who Bree's real father was. The idea that a stranger found out . . ." She swallowed hard, bothered by the thought.

"You'd be surprised at the kind of information he has access to." He sighed and shook his head. "I just need a moment."

Emily didn't say anything as she watched Austin step outside.

She would give him space . . . for now.

But she would take things into her own hands if they didn't make any progress finding Bree soon.

fifteen

AUSTIN HAD FELT a wide range of emotions today.

Surprise. Hope. Outrage.

There was more going on here than met the eye, and he needed to get to the bottom of things.

He stood outside the motel room, not wanting to go too far, and dialed his boss's number.

But there was no answer.

Except Larchmont *always* answered. So why wasn't he picking up now?

Austin would need to wait until later to find out. But he'd already lost so much time. Impatience churned inside him.

He put his phone away and let out a long breath before looking up at the sky, which was now dark.

All of this . . . it seemed surreal.

Part of him had always wanted to be a father. But he'd figured that wasn't likely to happen for him. Not with his job and his past, his upbringing even. He certainly hadn't had a great example of healthy family life. His dad was *not* a person Austin wanted to emulate.

He had his band of brothers at the agency. But they didn't fulfill the desire to have a family of his own.

Oh, God . . . He stared at the stars another moment. *Help me to do the right thing. Help me to sort my thoughts. Give me wisdom.*

Just as he looked back down, he spotted a black sedan driving slowly past the motel.

Something about the vehicle's pace caught his attention.

Why so slow?

Those men were inside, weren't they? They were looking for Emily.

Whoever wanted her dead was determined to succeed.

His jaw tightened at the thought.

Quickly, Austin slipped into the room and locked the door behind him.

"Austin?" Emily murmured.

He didn't answer.

Instead, he went to the window and nudged the curtain aside. He wanted to keep an eye on these guys. See if they pulled up to the motel.

To his dismay, a moment later, they drove into the lot.

Austin braced himself for whatever would happen next.

———

"WHAT'S WRONG?" Emily's voice wavered.

Austin's body language indicated something had happened—something worrisome.

He didn't even look back at her. He just continued facing the window.

"Someone suspicious pulled up, and I'm keeping an eye on them."

"What?" Her voice came out sounding raspy.

She thought his friends were keeping an eye on those guys. So who was outside right now?

When would this nightmare end?

"What are we going to do?" Emily wrapped her arms over her chest as she realized there was only one way in and out of this room. There were no balconies or even windows that could open. Only the front door.

And was there a *we*? Or was Trevor still taking over?

Emily wasn't clear on that yet.

Austin already had his phone to his ear and was talking to someone.

A moment later, he turned back to her. "Gage said that the guys at the house haven't gone anywhere."

"Wait, so you're saying these guys outside now aren't the same ones who shot at us earlier?" Had Emily read too much into things? Or were there more people than she'd realized trying to kill her?

"Whoever this is, they're clearly looking for someone." Austin kept his gaze focused outside, still not turning to look at her. "Maybe the mastermind behind this hired more people than we assumed."

Emily shivered again. She didn't like the sound of that.

"So instead of the two people trying to kill me, there could be four?" The words sounded surreal, even to her own ears.

Austin flickered his gaze over his shoulder before he quickly turned back to the window. "I don't know what's going on. But I'm going to keep my eye on these guys. If it comes down to it. I'll act."

At those words, Austin pulled the gun from his waist.

Then he angled himself toward the window and continued to watch.

sixteen

AUSTIN'S LUNGS WERE TIGHT. He hadn't expected anyone to show up here. Especially not since he had Gage watching the men who'd followed them earlier.

Maybe this was bigger than he'd ever imagined.

He was three seconds away from calling Trevor and telling him to come back.

"Well?" Emily's gentle voice cut into the tension thrumming through him.

He stared at the men. "They're walking along the outside of the motel as if they're looking for something . . . or someone."

"Are they knocking on the doors?" Her voice sounded more fragile now.

"No. That's good news."

"There's no way they should know we're here. I don't have a phone. You switched cars."

He backed into the shadows as one of the men glanced up at the second floor. "I suppose they could have put a tracker on my car earlier. It could have pinged here, even though it's not here anymore. So these guys could have come just to check it out."

"Are you going to let your colleague know?" Emily asked.

"I already texted Trevor. Right now, he's lying low."

Austin tensed as the men talked in the parking lot again.

A moment later, they climbed back into their car and pulled away.

Austin's shoulders softened but only for a moment.

This was far from being over.

He had to figure out what had happened to Bree . . . his daughter.

And he had to keep Emily safe.

That meant they didn't have any time to waste.

They had to figure out some answers.

Now.

EMILY WANTED TO FEEL RELIEF. Wanted to let down her guard. But she couldn't. Not with everything going on.

Austin finally put his gun away and moved back to his bed. Just like earlier, he sat on the edge of his mattress, and Emily sat on her bed across from him.

A safe distance.

"If we're going to find Bree, then I'm going to need to dig a little bit deeper," Austin started. "I need details."

Her heart pounded in her ears. "Does this mean you're not handing this over to Trevor?"

His gaze darkened. "No. This is personal now."

Emily didn't bother to hide the relief from her expression. "Right. I'll tell you anything you need to know."

He reached into his duffel and pulled out a piece of paper and a pen. "This could take a while."

"I've got as much time as you need. I just want to find my daughter . . . *our* daughter."

Austin flinched at her words, but she didn't hold him at fault for that.

It would take time for him to come to terms with that revelation.

He let out a quick breath before focusing his attention on her. "Okay, so you think your former father-in-law took her, right?"

She nodded, an image of Conrad filling her mind. The man was short, but he carried himself like a giant. He kept his hair shaved almost to the skin, and he dressed impeccably.

He and Paul had looked a lot alike.

He was in the business of commercial real estate. He bought up properties in the city and leased them out to various stores and businesses. He'd made millions doing so.

She told Austin all of that.

"And where does Mr. Rankin live?" Austin asked.

She rubbed her neck, which suddenly felt achy. "New York City."

Austin blinked. "New York City? You think he grabbed Bree and took her back there?"

Emily let out a long breath, the question feeling burdensome. "I didn't at first. But I've been trying to think things through—especially since I know now that Bree isn't at the house with those men. I wonder if Conrad had his guys take Bree and set the house on fire hoping I would die. Then I wonder if he had someone take her to New York."

A shadow came over his gaze. "From the sounds of it, he's a smart man. You don't think he fears getting caught? It's just a matter of time before the FBI will catch wind of this."

"Conrad is a man with many resources, including multiple homes. He'll have all of his bases covered. I'm sure he has a plan—though I have no idea what that plan is." Those facts scared her.

"I think we should pay him a visit."

Emily nodded. "He's supposed to return tomorrow from an overseas trip. I think visiting him is a great idea."

Austin paused, his thoughts clearly still churning. Finally, he asked, "Do you believe the threat the kidnapper sent you? That if you talk to the police, Bree will be killed?"

She swallowed hard as her limbs began to shake. "I can't afford not to."

seventeen

AUSTIN STUDIED EMILY'S FACE, wondering what she wasn't saying.

As far as he knew, the woman was above reproach. Not that he'd looked into her.

He'd tried to forget about her, for that matter.

Because she'd changed everything for him.

After he'd met Emily, Austin had realized he didn't want to be *that guy* anymore.

He didn't want to use women or drinking to relieve the stress he felt on his job. He needed to face his demons head-on instead of avoiding them by every means possible.

Too many people could get hurt by his actions.

So he'd turned his life around. Since then, he

hadn't touched alcohol. Hadn't dated at all—or had any more one-night stands.

He'd owned up to his responsibilities and poured himself into his work instead.

He'd even started going to church.

But Emily had remained in the back of his mind. He'd wondered how she was. What she was doing. If she'd ever settled down.

He'd never imagined any of this. Not in his wildest dreams.

"Emily . . ." His tone made it clear that he knew there was more to her story.

She closed her eyes before opening them again. Then she drew in a deep but shaky breath.

As Austin saw her struggling, he had the urge to reach out and comfort her. But he didn't dare. Especially not now. Not here.

Not that his touch would even be welcome.

He had more information, so now he needed to figure out a plan.

He wasn't sure, but he didn't think Emily had the means to pay for the expense of this investigation. It didn't come cheap.

But in Austin's mind, this all went back to Larchmont.

Who was that man who had given her the card?

Theories tried to form in Austin's mind, but he knew he shouldn't jump to conclusions.

For now, he needed to let Emily rest. She looked tired with the dark circles beneath her eyes and her unusually pale skin.

He doubted she'd gotten any rest since Bree had been taken.

But first thing in the morning, they needed to head to New York.

—————

EMILY LAY IN BED, thinking everything through.

She'd tried to get in touch with her former father-in-law three different times since the fire.

At first, his secretary claimed he was in a meeting. Then she'd said Conrad had left for a business trip. Wherever he'd gone, there was no cell service.

But Emily didn't believe a word the woman said.

Conrad was the only person who made sense as a kidnapper. He'd been resentful he hadn't been able to see Bree more since Paul's death. But Emily didn't think the man was a good influence.

Conrad was too focused on work. Too into materialism. At getting deals no matter the cost.

Plus, Bree wasn't his flesh and blood, and Conrad

knew that. Bree and Conrad had never even been especially close, and Bree had never bonded with the man.

But the thing about Conrad was that whatever Conrad wanted, Conrad got.

Would he have taken it so far as to have kidnapped Bree? To try to have Emily killed?

Emily's throat tightened at the thought, at the possible betrayal. But she wouldn't put it past the man.

He definitely had the money for it. The fact Conrad was supposedly out of town seemed like a perfect alibi, especially if he had other people to do his dirty work.

Maybe when he got back, she should confront him.

Demand answers.

Conrad wouldn't give her any information. Emily knew that. He'd never liked her. He'd never thought she was good enough for Paul, and he didn't bother to hide that fact.

But maybe Austin could convince him to talk. Austin, with his tall frame, broad shoulders, and deep voice. The only thing that didn't match his tough persona was the fact he liked flashy sports cars. But that also made him more interesting, Emily supposed.

Or at least it had at one time. Not anymore. Right now, the only thing she was concentrating on was Bree.

Even though the lights in the motel room were out, she slipped the picture of Bree from her pocket. The glow from the bathroom—they'd left the light on and opened the door just a slit—was enough for her to see the photo.

As she stared at her little girl's image, tears slipped down her cheeks. Bree's smile was so innocent and sweet. Her hair a light honey-blonde just like Emily's.

But her eyes . . . they were just like Austin's.

They were different colors, but they were the same shape and brightness. And the look in their gazes . . . it was mischievous yet serious at the same time.

A perfect match.

Certainly, Austin had been able to see that also.

Emily ran her fingers over the outline of her daughter's face.

I'll get you back, sweet girl. I'll get you back.

eighteen

AUSTIN AWOKE the next morning before the sun rose.

He had too much on his mind to sleep. Plus, he'd been keeping one ear open just in case any more trouble came their way.

He'd lain in bed quietly, but he'd heard Emily crying.

He almost didn't want to feel sorry for her. He wanted to be upset with her. To hold it against her that she'd kept Bree to herself all these years.

But none of this was her fault. Austin had set himself up to be a nameless stranger. He hadn't wanted Emily tracking him down. Hadn't wanted to be tied down. Hadn't wanted any type of commitment.

From the sound of it, Emily had tried to find him. Had exhausted every means possible, for that matter. Honestly, the lengths she'd gone through to find him were impressive.

So he truly had no reason to be upset with her.

In fact, maybe he was just upset with himself. For not being more responsible. For being reckless all those years ago.

Though he'd wised up and had a change of heart, that didn't mean he could erase what he'd done.

Bree was proof of that.

Not that he'd want to erase Bree.

He hadn't met the girl, but he couldn't wait to do so.

But first, he had to find her.

He slipped out of bed and cleaned himself up.

By the time he emerged from the bathroom, Emily was awake and standing at the sink. From all appearances, she'd washed her face, combed her hair, and brushed her teeth.

"Morning." The word came out sounding like a croak as she ran a finger underneath her eyes.

"Morning." Austin breezed past her toward the overnight bag he'd left on the bed.

Was this what it would have been like if he'd stuck around after their first night together? Would they have had a future? Eventually gotten married and settled into a nice routine as a couple?

But he hadn't stuck around. His MO had been to leave in the middle of the night.

He'd known facing the women he had one-night stands with the next morning would be too difficult. Would leave him too vulnerable.

Looking back, he'd been a total jerk. He wished he could change things . . . but that wasn't possible. He now had to live with his mistakes.

"We're going to New York today to track down Conrad," he finally said. "We should leave as soon as possible."

"I agree." Emily nodded at the bathroom. "I can be ready in ten minutes."

"That would be great," he told her. "We can pick up some breakfast on the way out."

She nodded again before closing the door.

He released his breath.

Good. He could use a little space from her.

Because being around Emily—and their conversation last night—had stirred up so many things inside him . . . and the result had left him feeling off his game.

In this situation, that was unacceptable.

———

EMILY STARTED the water in the bathroom but made no effort to get in the shower.

Instead, she pressed her forehead against the door.

Seeing Austin emerge from the bathroom with his hair wet and steam flowing out from behind him had set off a string of memories.

Not because she'd ever seen him emerge from the shower before. She hadn't.

The moment just felt intimate.

She'd been such an idiot seven years ago. The one time she decided to cut loose, she'd gone all out.

What had she been thinking?

After she and Austin had connected at the bar, she'd really thought there was more to him. Sure, she'd pegged him as a player. But she saw some hurt down deep inside him, and she'd wanted to know the cause. Had wanted to uncover who he really was.

Maybe, at the heart of things, she'd thought he would be different. That she could change him.

They'd had what felt like a real connection.

After their night together, she'd awoken bright-eyed the next morning.

She foolishly thought Austin would still be in bed beside her. That they could talk. That maybe he'd felt the same thing she did. That, even though this was just supposed to be a fling, there could be more to it.

Instead, he'd been gone. He hadn't even left a note. Hadn't even said goodbye.

Regret had instantly filled her. She'd cried. Beat herself up for her rash decisions. Prayed for forgiveness. Wondered why anyone ever did things like this.

Then she'd tried to forget about what had happened.

Until she'd found out she was pregnant.

Then there was no forgetting.

When she met Paul, he'd seemed like an answer to prayer. He had a good job. A stable lifestyle. He wanted to settle down.

He hadn't minded the fact Emily was pregnant with another man's baby. At least, he hadn't seemed to mind at first. The truth had come out later, mostly in heated arguments where he'd accused Emily of giving Bree too much attention.

He hadn't been an answer to prayer.

He'd been another mistake.

For someone who always tried to do things right, Emily had done an awful lot wrong.

Finally, she forced herself to straighten then hopped in the shower.

She prayed that once she and Austin got to New York, they'd be able to find some answers.

She would give up everything to get her daughter

back. She'd give up her own freedoms. Her own rights. Her own happiness.

Everything.

She just needed to know that her daughter was safe.

nineteen

AUSTIN GRIPPED the steering wheel as he and Emily headed down the road.

The SUV wasn't nearly as exciting as the Mustang convertible.

But the vehicle was reliable and safe—and it didn't stand out in a sea of other vehicles.

He and Emily had already grabbed some biscuits from a fast-food restaurant, along with coffee.

The two of them hadn't had much to say to each other on the drive, but that was fine by him.

His mind raced through what they'd need to do once they arrived. He'd find Conrad. Question him. Keep Emily safe.

Each seemed like a monumental task.

"How did you get those scars?" Emily's voice cut into his thoughts.

He glanced at his arm. His shirt sleeve had pulled up, revealed a set of pale lines on his forearm.

He swallowed hard and tugged his sleeve down. "Military."

She'd asked him about those scars seven years ago also. He'd made up some flimsy excuse about an accident. Clearly, she'd seen through his lies.

"Part of a mission I was on," he finally said.

"Did they torture you or something?"

He said nothing.

"I'm sorry." She placed her hand on his shoulder and closed her eyes. "I shouldn't have asked that."

"It's okay. It's just not something I like to talk about."

"I get it."

She removed her hand, and Austin instantly missed her touch.

Which was crazy. He had no business craving a connection with her.

With anyone.

When he'd signed up for Project Elevate, he knew that meant basically being a hermit for the rest of his life. That was how it felt, anyway.

Like he was created to be that way.

Like it was his lot in life, so he needed to accept it.

But what if man truly wasn't meant to be alone?

How would Bree change that?

As soon as they pulled into the city, Emily straightened. Her gaze wandered up to the skyscrapers surrounding them. To the traffic coming at them from every direction. At the throngs of people on the sidewalks and crossing the streets.

"Are you nervous because of what we're about to do or because of the city?" Austin asked.

She released a breath, her shoulders relaxing ever so slightly. "A little bit of both, I guess. I have never been much of a city girl, even though I lived here for several years. It's why living outside Lancaster has been perfect for me." She let out a self-deprecating laugh. "I know what you're probably thinking—that it seems weird that someone who helps people with their mental health has so much anxiety herself."

"That's not what I'm thinking at all."

She stole a glance at him, not bothering to hide the surprise in her eyes. "Really? Because I feel like that's what most people think."

"Maybe I'm not most people. We all have things we struggle with. I'm sure you know that as a counselor. What would you tell your patients?"

She drew in a long breath before slowly releasing it.

"That it's important to acknowledge our issues in order to move forward."

"Sounds like good advice."

Austin glanced at his GPS. They were almost there. Thankfully, he found a parallel parking space on the side of the road. That would make this a little easier.

He pulled into the space and cut the engine before turning to Emily.

This was the moment they would find some answers.

Austin hoped they did, for all their sakes.

———

EMILY'S CHEST felt so tight that she was certain air wasn't getting to her lungs.

She hadn't been to this building in a long time. She'd told herself she never wanted to come here again. Yet here she was.

Conrad Rankin's office took up the entirety of the twelfth floor here at Cabot Towers.

Rankin Enterprises was one of the top businesses in the city, and Paul had been poised to take over. He'd spent probably twelve hours a day here, trying to impress his father and get ahead.

Emily had overheard some of Paul's business deals—and she hadn't approved. When she'd asked Paul about them, he'd brushed her off. Said she wouldn't understand.

He hadn't even bothered to explain—almost as if she were too stupid to comprehend the deals. But secretly, he'd wanted her to feel stupid. It was a subtle mind game with devastating consequences.

He'd been charming at first.

It wasn't until they were married for three years that his true colors had emerged.

It was one thing when he'd been impatient with Emily. But when he started getting short with Bree, Emily had spoken out.

Paul hadn't liked that side of her. That, combined with his stress from work, had made for a turbulent relationship.

Now, she needed to face her demons again, specifically one named Conrad Rankin.

She started to reach for the door handle when Austin grabbed her arm.

"Hey," he started.

She jerked her gaze toward his. "Yes?"

"I know this isn't what you want to hear," he started, his tone apologetic. "But I need to go in there alone."

"What?" Resistance gripped her. "No, absolutely not—"

"Hear me out first. From what I understand about your relationship with Conrad, it's not a good one. I don't want him to shut down or to think you're playing him. If I can talk to him and explain this on a logical level, then I hope I can get some answers that way."

Every part of Emily rebelled. But she inhaled a deep breath and tried to think the situation through rationally.

She didn't want to do anything to jeopardize her daughter. However, she'd never been in a situation like this before and didn't know the best way to proceed. Her emotions clouded her judgment.

Did Austin's words make sense? He was the professional here.

At the same time, Emily was supposed to be an expert on human behavior. What if she could spot something in Conrad's conduct that Austin couldn't?

Austin's gaze locked with hers. "You've got to trust me. Now that I know I'm Bree's father, you've got to know I also want what is best for her."

He had a point. That was why Emily had wanted Austin to help her and not Trevor.

Austin wasn't going into this as a total stranger. He had a stake in the situation now.

Yet he'd never met Bree, so he couldn't possibly care for her as much as Emily did. Maybe that wasn't a fair statement. She wasn't sure. She was too jittery to think clearly.

Emily sucked in a deep breath and held it before slowly releasing it.

Then she nodded. "Okay. You go in first. But if you don't get the answers we need, then I'm going in next."

twenty

AUSTIN STEPPED into the office building and mentally prepared himself for the upcoming conversation.

He couldn't blow this. He felt more pressure than ever for this mission to succeed.

Because now this was personal.

He remembered the picture Emily had shown him of Bree.

His beautiful little girl.

He desperately wanted to get to know her. To see if she was anything like him.

Could the two of them have a relationship in the future? If Austin had anything to do with it, they would. He wouldn't leave his daughter without a father. Not if he could help it.

That realization gave him the motivation he needed to keep moving forward.

He smiled at the security guard near the door and then glanced down at his clothes. He'd tried to dress for the occasion, knowing that his usual jeans and T-shirt wouldn't cut it in this environment. Instead, he'd worn khakis with a button-up black top. The outfit wasn't much better, but it was a start.

Based on what Emily had told him, Conrad's secretary had indicated the man should be getting back from his trip today.

If any of that was true.

Austin had asked his colleagues to look into the man, but they hadn't found much information. Conrad probably used a private jet to travel, which made finding out information much more difficult. They had confirmed he had some property in South America, however.

Men with resources like those Conrad had could hide much more easily. Their personal security and well-being relied on privacy.

As Austin waited for the elevator, his phone buzzed. He glanced at it, hoping to see Larchmont's name. His boss still hadn't called him back.

But it wasn't Larchmont. It was just a spammer.

He scowled and shoved the phone back into his pocket.

Why hadn't Larchmont returned his calls? It was unlike him—and it made Austin suspicious.

Austin needed to call his boss again, but he'd wait until after this meeting. He wanted to be able to focus fully on everything Conrad Rankin said.

He hoped this conversation proved to be fruitful.

He got off the elevator on the twelfth floor and plastered on a smile as he approached the receptionist.

As he did, Austin prayed for good results.

———

EMILY'S GAZE continued to dart around her at the busy urban streets.

What she'd told Austin had been the truth. She wasn't much of a city girl. All the busyness, the movement coming from every direction, the honking horns, the constant buzz . . . it didn't settle her soul. The unceasing activity did the opposite.

Right now, her anxiety felt like a siren endlessly wailing in her soul. As hard as she tried, she couldn't silence it.

Was Austin talking to Conrad yet? Or was the man

still out of town? Had he really been out of town like his secretary said?

If Conrad did have Bree, did that mean her daughter was being kept at his house? Who was watching her? Hopefully not those thugs he'd hired.

Emily swallowed hard and pulled her arms over her chest, desperate for some type of comfort. The questions only badgered her more and added to her anxiety.

Conrad's wife, Maria, had died four years ago of cancer. The man now lived at a massive estate on the outskirts of New York City all by himself. Except for his hired staff, of course.

Paul had been his only son.

If Emily knew one thing, it was that the man's grief was real. Losing both Paul and his wife had been devastating.

Even though Emily didn't like the man, she had felt sorry for him. Losing loved ones was so incredibly hard. That kind of grief wasn't something she'd wish on her worst enemy.

Her gaze stopped on someone standing on the corner across the street. She didn't know why, out of all the people on the street, this man had caught her eye.

Was it because he was wearing all black? Plenty of people did that.

It wasn't how he looked or dressed. It was his body language, she realized.

Something about the way he lingered on the corner. About the way he occasionally glanced at her. About how he looked almost too casual.

Because of his sunglasses, Emily couldn't say for sure the man was watching her. But she sensed he was.

Was he one of the men from last night? Had he followed her and Austin here? She squinted, trying to see if she could recognize him. But he was too far away. Besides, she hadn't really gotten a good look at the men last night either.

She'd seen Austin check in the rearview mirror on the drive. Surely, he would have known it if someone was tailing them.

She shivered, suddenly feeling exposed. Like she was stuck in this vehicle with nowhere to go. No keys, so she couldn't drive away. No phone. No weapon, even though she wouldn't know how to use it.

No, she was a figurative sitting duck.

Her pulse pounded in her ears.

She couldn't just stay here and wait for these men to do something. She had to act before it was too late.

twenty-one

"I'M SORRY, were we supposed to meet?" Conrad Rankin stared at Austin as they stood in his office.

The room had green marble walls, fine leather furniture, and various pieces of artwork featuring men playing cricket. Those paintings probably cost more than many people's homes.

Austin was thankful he'd made it this far. Surprisingly, the receptionist hadn't given him a hard time. He'd mentioned Bree just as Conrad walked in.

Austin instantly had his interest.

"No, we don't have a meeting," Austin explained. "But it's of utmost importance that I speak with you."

Conrad set his briefcase on his desk. "As you can see, I literally just this moment got back to my office.

I've been out of the country. You mentioned my granddaughter. Is she okay?"

"We believe she's been kidnapped."

Conrad's eyes widened, and he froze behind his desk. "What? What do you mean kidnapped?"

"Emily's house was set on fire. When she went to get Bree from her room, the girl was missing."

"There was a fire?" An unreadable emotion flared to life in his eyes.

"That's right."

"Arson?" he continued.

"They don't know yet."

He was silent a moment before asking, "And you think Bree's been taken?"

Conrad's tone certainly didn't sound like that of a guilty man. He sounded truly shocked.

Austin nodded. "That's correct. Then Emily got a text saying she shouldn't tell law enforcement that Bree was missing. That if she didn't comply they would kill her daughter."

Emily had given him permission to say that much.

"She didn't even tell the cops?" Conrad reached for the phone on his desk as if he were about to do it himself.

Austin snatched the device from his hands. "You can't make that call."

Conrad stared at him, not bothering to hide the contempt in his gaze. "She's my granddaughter. Of *course* I can."

"But Bree isn't really your granddaughter," Austin reminded him. He hadn't wanted to play that card, but he needed the upper hand here.

Conrad's gaze darkened. "Who are you again?"

Austin considered what approach to take. Should he admit he was Bree's father? Or should he only share that he'd been hired to find her? Which would have the most impact?

"I've been hired to find her. And . . . I'm her father." He decided to dive in with both of those facts.

Conrad blinked several times as if trying to be certain Austin was telling the truth.

Then his shoulders slumped, and he shook his head. "I want to deny it, but I can see the resemblance. And I resent you saying that I'm not actually her grandfather just because we're not blood-related. I've been in her life since she was born."

Austin inwardly flinched at the remark, but he maintained his composure. His words had been a power play, but part of him regretted throwing that fact in the man's face.

"My apologies," Austin said. "But I'm trying to figure out if I can rule you out as a suspect."

Conrad pointed to himself and let out a cynical laugh. "Me? You think I would have taken my own granddaughter?"

"Apparently, you were very upset because Emily didn't let you see Bree enough."

"Well, yes! Of course! That doesn't mean I'd kidnap her. I'd never want any harm to come to that sweet girl." Conrad stared at Austin, an incredulous look on his face. "I wouldn't set her house on fire and take the girl. That insinuation is preposterous!"

Austin stared at the man, trying to figure out if he was telling the truth or not.

Because if he was . . . then he and Emily's best lead had just been marked off their list.

———

THAT MAN HAD DEFINITELY GLANCED her way, Emily mused.

Not only had he glanced at her, but he was up to something.

She shifted in her seat, unable to get comfortable. She wasn't sure how much longer she could stay in the SUV.

At any moment, she expected the man to show up

at her window. To show her a hidden gun. To direct her to come with him or else.

That scenario would only end one way.

With her dead.

Those men already tried to kill her in the fire. Tried to shoot her when she left that café. Had tried to track her down at her old house and the motel.

These guys weren't going to stop.

This is no time to be reactive, she told herself. You need to be proactive.

Emily knew all kinds of ways to emotionally survive tragedies.

But physically surviving danger? Definitely not her area of expertise.

She glanced around, desperate to figure out a plan. People milled all around—shoppers, businessmen and women, tourists. Traffic was bumper-to-bumper with so many horns being honked—almost as if doing so were as natural as breathing. Skyscrapers loomed over her, salesmen tried to sell hats and purses on the corner, and a small stand sold hot dogs on the other side of the street.

Another man on the corner across the street caught her eye—a man dressed in black, wearing sunglasses, simply lingering with his phone to his ear.

Her heart ratcheted even faster.

There were two of them, she realized. Two men were watching her.

She had a better chance of losing these guys in a crowd than she did by sitting here waiting for Austin to return.

If she did wait, she feared by the time Austin got back, she'd either be abducted herself . . . or dead.

She made a quick decision.

As a firetruck wailed in the distance, she hopped into the back seat of the SUV, and then into the cargo area.

Carefully, she hit the latch button and popped open the back hatch—but only lifted it as much as absolutely necessary.

She slunk out, and her feet landed on the concrete.

Carefully, she closed the hatch behind her.

Then she rose and glanced in front of her. The two men shouldn't be able to see her from this angle. They were located on the two street corners in front of the SUV.

But she didn't have much time.

She could run fast and furious, but that would only draw attention.

The best thing she could do right now was to walk away. To blend in. To look casual.

She pulled her hoodie over her head. Then she jammed her hands in the pockets.

Lifting a quick prayer, she started walking in the opposite direction.

She prayed those men didn't see her.

Please, God. Please. Not for my sake but for Bree's . .

.

twenty-two

"I **ASSURE** you I would never do anything to harm Bree." Conrad stiffened as he stood by his desk, casting an icy glare on Austin. "Sure, I want to see her more. It's very important to me to spend time with her. But I also know that Emily has a lot of things to work out."

What did that mean? Austin wondered. He wasn't about to ask. Not right now.

Instead, he waited for Conrad to continue.

Conrad sat in his office chair—and he sat down hard, almost as if his legs had given out. His motions appeared stiff with shock, and his eyes suddenly looked hollow.

"My wife and I tried to raise Paul to be a good person. But somewhere down the road, we failed him. I was in denial about it for years. Until one day, Bree told me about some of the interactions she'd seen between Emily and Paul. That's when I knew Paul wasn't treating Emily well. I sat him down, and we had a long talk. I really hoped things had changed after that. But I don't think they did."

Had Paul been abusing Emily? She hadn't mentioned that in their conversation.

Heat rushed through Austin's veins at the thought.

Emily had deserved so much better than what life had handed her. But Austin had no room to judge Paul. Well, maybe *a little* room. What Austin had done to Emily was terrible in its own right. Neither of them had treated her well.

How could Austin show her he was a new person? That he'd changed? That he'd lived so long with shame and regret, but now he was different?

He wasn't sure he could.

He swallowed hard as he turned his focus back on Conrad. "Do you have any idea who might have taken her? Who might want Emily dead?"

"Someone's trying to kill Emily?" More surprise laced his voice. "You mean in the house fire?"

"There's been more than one attempt on her life."

"Who would want to harm—" Conrad shook his head as if an idea hit him.

"If you know something, you have to tell me." Austin stepped closer, his voice edged with seriousness. "More than one life is on the line right now."

Conrad ran a hand over his face. Hesitated another moment. Blew out a breath.

Then he slowly nodded. "I hate to say it, but Paul made some bad business deals. He acquired a lot of enemies in the process. I've tried to clean up a bunch of his messes, but I haven't always been successful."

"Do you have a particular name in mind?"

Conrad hesitated another moment before nodding. "Peyton Martin. He's one of our biggest competitors, and Paul got a land deal that Peyton desperately wanted—and thought should be his. He made Paul's life miserable afterward."

"Miserable how?"

"He started some rumors about Paul in the business world—how he was underhanded and couldn't be trusted. Sometimes in real estate, all you've got is your reputation. Peyton sent Emily photos of Paul with another woman and claimed Paul was cheating on her."

Austin wanted to be surprised, but he wasn't. "Was he cheating?"

Conrad's gaze clouded. "He wasn't seeing that woman."

Austin noticed how he didn't say Paul wasn't cheating, however. Austin had met Paul's type before. Men like him thought they deserved everything they wanted—business deals, money, women.

Disgust roiled in his stomach.

"Anything else?" Austin asked.

"Those were the biggest things." Conrad let out a long breath. "But Peyton had a real chip on his shoulder."

"Why would he take revenge on Emily and Bree? Wasn't Paul the one he had hard feelings toward?"

Conrad lifted a shoulder in a half shrug. "He wanted what Paul had."

"Including his wife and daughter?" The idea seemed too outlandish. Would the man really take things that far? He had a hard time envisioning it.

"Emily? He probably thinks of her as an obstacle to getting what he wants. But Bree . . . Peyton would see her as a prize." Conrad's gaze hardened. "If he has my granddaughter . . ."

He didn't have to finish his statement. Part of Austin didn't want to hear aloud what he would say. He knew.

"I'll check him out." Austin took a step back.

"I can pay you to find her. Or hire people to help you. Whatever you need. I need for Bree to be found."

Austin shook his head. "I want to keep my circle small right now. I have to know who I can trust."

"I feel like we should call the police or the FBI." Conrad twisted his neck and gave Austin a side glance as he waited for his response.

"I will call them if I need to." Austin locked his gaze on Conrad's. "You have my word. But if you call them yourself, you could put Bree's life in danger. Unfortunately, we're playing by the kidnappers' rules right now, and if we get out of line, I'm not sure what they'll do."

Conrad stared at him another moment before nodding. "I understand. I won't call. Not yet. Please, let me know what happens. I know you may not have a high opinion of me, and neither may Emily, but I truly do only want what's best for them."

The man sounded sincere.

But Austin knew better than to trust him.

He would need to be very careful how he proceeded.

* * *

EMILY TRIED NOT to look back over her shoulder. The action might draw attention. It might even make her look too suspicious.

But as soon as she ducked around the corner of the office building, she paused. Slowly, she leaned toward the edge and peered around.

One of those men . . . he stood beside her SUV, staring inside.

She'd gotten out just in time.

When he realized Emily wasn't inside, he would begin searching for her.

She turned back toward the street.

Should she duck inside the building beside her or stay on the sidewalk?

She had to decide quickly. She had no time to waste.

She hurried past the office building where Austin was. She didn't trust that it was safe inside. What if Conrad had his men stationed somewhere in there, watching for her?

It was too risky.

Instead, she ducked around the other corner.

She continued walking when an idea hit her.

It might not pay off. But maybe it was worth a chance.

She reached the other corner and then headed left.

She was essentially headed back to the area where those men had been.

If her suspicions were correct, then those two men

would branch out to search for her in the other direction.

It was like playing a game of tag with Bree. Her daughter's trick had always been to hide close, wait for the person who was "it" to walk away, and then circle back around to homebase.

Finally, Emily reached the corner—the very one where one of those men had been standing only moments ago.

She didn't see those two guys anywhere.

Had she truly lost them?

She couldn't be sure.

Whatever she did, she had to remain on guard . . . even as panic tried to take hold.

twenty-three

AUSTIN EMERGED from the building and headed back to the SUV.

He reached it and froze.

Emily wasn't inside.

His pulse pounded harder.

Where had she gone? Had those men found her? Had they taken her?

Maybe leaving her out here had been a terrible idea after all.

And she still didn't have a new cell phone to call him if she needed help.

He glanced around, looking for a sign to indicate what had happened.

Across the street, he spotted one of the men who'd

been outside the hotel last night. He was sure it was the same man.

Austin's spine stiffened.

Somehow, those guys had managed to find him and Emily here.

How had they done that? Austin and Emily hadn't been followed this morning. He'd made sure of it.

It didn't matter right now. Austin had to find Emily.

At least she wasn't with that man. He still seemed to be searching for her.

Austin's gut told him Emily had seen those men and run.

But where would she go?

He turned away before the man saw him. Quickly, he bought a Yankees baseball cap from a nearby vendor, pulled it over his head, and walked in the opposite direction.

He couldn't let anything happen to Emily. Couldn't let things end this way. They'd just now reconnected, and he felt like they still had too many conversations to have.

Besides, he'd made a promise, and he intended to keep it.

Plus, Bree needed a mom.

His list of reasons could go on and on.

Just as he rounded the corner, he spotted someone ahead.

Was that . . . Emily? He thought it was. But the hood she had pulled over her head made it difficult to know for sure.

As she glanced over her shoulder, Austin caught a glimpse of her profile.

It was her.

She was okay.

Relief washed through him.

She was about to cross the street.

He hurried to catch up, quickly closing the space between them. "Emily!"

She paused and turned, fear lacing her eyes.

Then she saw him and released the breath she held. "Austin. Those men—"

"I know. I saw them." He took her elbow and kept walking, knowing they had no time to waste. "This way."

He pulled her toward a nearby subway entrance.

This location wasn't ideal, but it was the best way to put the most distance between them and those men.

He quickly bought two MetroCards and then hurried with Emily through the turnstile.

Then they waited at the platform for the train to arrive.

Austin glanced at the stairway, expecting to see the men emerge.

But they didn't. Not yet.

"I'm sorry." Emily sounded breathless as she stood stiffly beside him. "But I saw them, and I knew I couldn't stay in the SUV."

"You did the right thing. But we're not out of danger yet."

"I know." Her voice sounded thin.

Someone at the top of the stairway leading down into the subway caught his eye.

One of the men.

He'd found them.

And he was coming this way.

"Austin . . ." Emily's voice trembled.

He grabbed her arm as adrenaline surged through him. "I know. I see him."

The train stopped in front of them. As soon as the doors opened, he pulled Emily inside.

But not before Austin heard the man behind him shout, "Hey!"

———

EMILY'S HEART lodged in her throat with enough force she could hardly breathe.

How did these guys keep finding them?

Austin pulled her onto the subway car. It was already crowded with people, most of whom weren't paying any attention to anything around them.

They would be soon.

Wasting no time, Austin ran, tugging Emily through car after car.

People grumbled around them. Scowled. Made lewd comments.

But Emily and Austin didn't slow down. They continued running through the train.

She didn't dare look back, but she sensed the man closing in. Heard people muttering more obscenities toward them.

What were she and Austin going to do? How would they get out of this? Eventually, the subway cars would end, and they'd be stuck with this man.

They were almost at the front of the train.

Emily's veins felt like they could explode from apprehension.

"Stand clear of the closing doors, please," the recorded announcement said overhead.

They were about to be trapped on the subway with a killer closing in.

Suddenly, all of this seemed like a terrible idea.

They were going to die on this train, weren't they?

twenty-four

"THIS WAY!" Austin pulled Emily through the doors of the subway train just before they closed.

They paused for only a moment on the platform.

Then Austin glanced back, desperate to see if his plan worked.

The gunman had his face pressed into the glass. He mouthed something Austin couldn't hear, but he imagined the man's words.

Threats. Deadly promises. Vulgar names.

As much as Austin would like to take a breather, there was no time. There were two men.

He wasn't sure where the other man was.

He continued to pull Emily through the subway station, not slowing down.

"Austin?" Her voice sounded breathless behind him.

"We've got this," he called over his shoulder. "Just keep moving."

He darted across the platform to another train and pulled her through the open doors. But he still didn't let down his guard.

He found an empty seat and let Emily take it. Then he stood beside her and watched everyone coming and going on the train to make sure no one else had followed them.

He didn't see anyone, but he needed to be certain.

"Austin?" Emily repeated.

Finally, when the doors closed, he sat beside her.

"There's a good chance the first guy—the one who got stuck on that other subway train—called the second guy to let him know we'd gotten off on this platform," Austin explained. "I didn't want him looking for us there. We'll go a couple of stops to be sure we lose them."

Understanding rolled over her features, and she nodded quickly. "Smart thinking."

"Did you recognize that guy?" Austin thought he knew the answer to that question, but he wanted to ask anyway. They were the men he'd seen at the motel last night.

But Emily hadn't really gotten a good look at them. He wondered if they might be familiar and spark some ideas in her.

She shook her head. "I've never seen him before."

He nodded. "They're persistent, to say the least."

"Very."

Her gaze continued to dart around nervously.

There was nothing Austin could say to comfort her right now. The best thing he could do was to keep her safe.

A couple of stops later, he took her hand again and led her off the subway. Just as before, he scanned the station.

He didn't see any signs of danger. He may have truly lost those guys—for now, at least.

Yet those two were obviously tracking Austin and Emily. But how? Austin needed to figure that out.

They climbed a set of stairs to the street above, and he glanced around.

This was exactly where he'd wanted to go.

Emily stared at the business names on the storefronts as realization rolled over her. "Chinatown?"

A wrinkle of confusion formed on her brow as if she hadn't expected this stop.

"I thought we could grab a bite to eat," Austin

said. "Let things die down a bit. Then we'll figure out how to proceed."

Her shoulders relaxed, and she shrugged. "Now that you mention it, I *am* getting a little hungry."

He headed down the street to one of his favorite restaurants—Yue's Sichuan Cuisine. He'd spent quite a bit of time in New York on some assignments, so he was familiar with the area. He liked to come here whenever he was in town.

Though the Shadow Agency was based out of a small town near Lansing, Michigan, there was something about the city he also loved. He wouldn't want to live here, but visiting on occasion was thrilling.

The inside of Yue's was decorated with typical Asian fare—oriental fans on the wall, lanterns as lights, Asian fabrics as curtains over doorways, and red walls that gave the place a warm feel.

But it was the aroma in the air that made Austin feel at home. The smell of spicy peppers and deep-fried chicken and savory rice.

They were seated immediately, and Austin sat facing the doorway so he could see any trouble coming.

Then he glanced at Emily, knowing she was anxious for an update.

However, he wasn't sure she would like what he had to say.

EMILY WANTED to enjoy her dry-braised chicken and potatoes—Austin's recommendation. But she was eating purely for nourishment and energy right now. She was sure it tasted good, but there was nothing she'd enjoy.

"So you don't think my father-in-law is behind this?" She could hardly believe the words were leaving her mouth. Because Conrad had been the only person who made sense.

"He seemed sincerely surprised when he heard Bree had been taken. I had my guys check. He was out of town." Austin picked up a piece of his General Tso's and took a bite.

"But he could have hired someone—"

"It didn't sound to me as if he wanted to traumatize Bree." Austin paused with his chopsticks in the air. "I'm not saying he's not guilty. But my gut instinct tells me he's innocent."

Emily nibbled on her lip as she tried to comprehend that. She'd been certain Conrad was the one behind this. "Who could it be then?"

Austin shifted, his gaze scanning out the window again—no doubt watching for those guys to come. "He did suggest somebody else."

She set her fork down and straightened with anticipation. "Who?"

"A man named Peyton Martin." Austin watched her expression.

"Peyton?" Her eyes narrowed. "He was an acquaintance of Paul's."

"I heard they didn't have a great relationship."

"Conrad told you that?" She frowned but nodded. "No, they didn't. They had an unhealthy rivalry. It was almost as if winning at the real estate game was a display of survival of the fittest. I think they both took their antics too far."

"Sounds like their competitiveness could have been dangerous."

"Maybe." She frowned again. "But I just don't know if I could see Peyton taking it as far as to kidnap Bree and make these threats."

"Maybe Paul had something Peyton wants. Speaking of which, we need to get you a new phone so you can check your messages. I'll need to make sure the new device is untraceable, however."

"I'd feel better if I had a cell with me. That way I could call you instead of taking off in a run at the first sign of trouble."

Austin lowered his voice to an almost intimate

tone. "I know that was a hard decision to make, but you made the right one."

Emily took a long sip of water, suddenly parched. She wasn't sure why she was relishing in Austin's affirmation. But something about his words made her heart do a flip.

"Do you know where Peyton is now?" Austin asked when she set her glass down.

"Last I heard, he was living in a sizable estate in the Hamptons." She paused. "Maybe we should pay him a visit."

Austin nodded slowly, almost as if he'd been waiting for her to suggest that. "A visit could be a good idea."

He reached into his wallet, pulled out some cash, and dropped it on the table.

Then he stood. "But first, let's go get you a phone."

twenty-five

AUSTIN FOUND the store he wanted and purchased a phone for Emily.

The device wasn't cheap, and Emily had mentioned something to him about money. But he wasn't too concerned with funding right now. After all, Bree was his daughter too.

Every time he remembered that fact, shock washed over him. It still seemed so unbelievable that he was a dad.

But he thought Emily was telling the truth—especially when he saw Bree's picture.

He couldn't believe he'd missed out all these years. All because of some stupid decision he'd made not to get attached to anyone.

Given his job, he supposed it might make sense. But still . . .

As the clerk—who just happened to be one of Austin's contacts and a tech genius—worked to set up Emily's phone, Austin's cell rang. He glanced at the screen and saw it was Larchmont—finally, the man was calling him back.

Austin excused himself to take the call, anxious to hear what his boss had to say.

He put the phone to his ear, his gaze still scanning the sidewalk in front of the store through the window. "Hey, there you are."

"You called?" Larchmont sounded all business.

"I did." Austin's voice was stiffer than normal. "You didn't answer, which is unusual."

"I had some personal matters to attend to. What's going on?"

Personal matters? That was the first time Austin ever remembered his boss mentioning anything about a life outside the Shadow Agency.

Austin glanced back at Emily. She stared out the window, a pensive expression on her face. The woman was the picture of beauty and grace. He'd known from the moment they met that she was special.

If only he hadn't blown it. He doubted she'd ever give him another chance now.

He ignored the rush of affection and turned back to his conversation with Larchmont. Before he asked his most pressing questions, Austin gave Larchmont an update on the situation and requested he find them a vehicle so they could get out of the city. Going back to the SUV was too risky. Those men were most likely watching it.

"I'll take care of it. Is there anything else?" Larchmont asked.

Austin's muscles tightened. "Did you give Emily a card for the Shadow Agency?"

"What?" Surprise laced his former commander's voice.

"You heard me. Did you give Emily our card? Did you find her and let her know we might be able to help her?"

Larchmont let out a quick, irritated chuckle. "Why would I do that?"

"That's what I'm wondering also."

Any amusement faded from his voice. "No, I didn't. Now, what is this about?"

Austin still wasn't convinced, but he moved forward with the conversation anyway. "Someone gave Emily our card. They wanted her to connect with us for this assignment. And I think it was you."

"I don't solicit business. We have enough that

comes to us. Now, do you want to explain yourself?" His voice turned crisp and cold.

Austin stared at Emily another moment as she stood at the counter talking to the clerk helping with her cell phone. He thought about everything she'd been through. His part in it all.

"The missing girl . . ." Austin gripped his phone harder. "She's my daughter."

"What?" Larchmont blurted.

"It was a one-night stand many years ago. I didn't give Emily my name. I had no idea a pregnancy was the outcome. But I can't believe it's a coincidence Emily and I have reconnected after all these years."

"I'm inclined to agree," Larchmont said. "But it wasn't me. I had nothing to do with this."

Doubt churned inside Austin.

Larchmont *might* be telling the truth. But he might not be.

Either way, Austin was nearly certain his boss was still hiding something.

But what? Had Larchmont known about Bree? Wouldn't his boss have told Austin?

The questions fluttered in his head. He'd need to get to the bottom of those issues.

Right now, Emily turned back to him, phone in hand, waving it triumphantly.

"I've got to go," Austin muttered.

"We'll talk later."

Yes, they would, Austin mused. This conversation was far from over.

———

EMILY HAD OVERHEARD bits and pieces of Austin's conversation.

His tone sounded tense, and she was curious what had been said. All Austin had told her was that he'd been speaking with his boss.

He paid for the phone and then programmed it to have her calls and texts forwarded to this new device. The new phone was untraceable.

Still in the store, Austin huddled close and looked at her phone as it loaded.

Emily's hands trembled so badly as she held the device that she could hardly see the screen as her messages loaded.

Austin cupped his hand under hers to steady her.

Electricity surged through her at his touch, but she tried to ignore the feeling.

The sparks were definitely there, however.

From the moment they'd met, there had been something charged and exciting between them. They'd had a connection unlike Emily had ever felt before. She'd blamed those feelings on endorphins and having too much to drink.

But, even after all these years and without any alcohol in her system, she still felt the connection between them.

The phone screen loaded. Emily sighed, welcoming the distraction from her thoughts.

A voicemail popped up. She squinted as she hit a button, and a transcription of the message filled her screen.

> This is Fire Inspector Garnet in Lancaster. I need to talk to you about the fire. We've narrowed down the origin, and it appears an accelerant was used. We've now declared this an arson. I need to ask you some questions. Call me ASAP.

"Arson?" Austin murmured. "I guess you're not surprised."

She frowned. "No, I'm not."

An accelerant was used? Maybe Conrad wasn't guilty.

She hadn't told Austin that part of her story. Hadn't told him that Paul died in a fire also.

She knew how it looked. Knew what he'd think.

And she couldn't bring herself to talk about it.

She skimmed her texts until she stopped on one.

Her gaze hovered on the unknown number, but she hesitated to click it.

"That's it." Her voice quivered. "It's a message from the kidnappers."

"You want me to read it first?" Austin asked softly.

She considered his offer only a second before shaking her head. "No, I've got this."

With trembling fingers, she clicked on the message, and a text filled the screen.

> Back off, and she'll stay safe.

Her heart thrummed in her ears.

She looked up at Austin. "What should I do? Should I respond?"

His jaw hardened but he nodded and told her what to say.

She typed his words.

> What do you want from me?

Her throat tightened as she waited for their response.

Finally, it appeared.

Only for you to leave Bree alone.

A cry escaped from somewhere deep inside her. "I don't understand . . . why would they want to keep her? It doesn't make sense. I'll do anything to get her back."

"Ask for a picture of her so we can know she's okay," Austin muttered.

Emily's hands trembled as she typed the words.

The next thirty seconds felt like eternity. Finally, the sender replied with a photo.

Tears dripped from Emily's eyes when she saw the picture of Bree sitting on a carpeted floor holding a teddy bear and staring at the camera.

She didn't even look scared.

No, she looked defiant.

That was Bree for you.

Emily might laugh, but she couldn't. Not now. Not given these circumstances.

"Ask them again what they want." Austin's voice contained a new pensiveness as well.

It was hard for him to see this knowing what he did now, wasn't it? He saw Bree in a new light.

Emily quickly typed her reply.

> What do you want in return for her?

But there was nothing.

No reply.

No dots indicating the sender was typing something.

Another cry caught in Emily's throat. Her fears had been confirmed. Austin had been right. They weren't going to make demands.

They just wanted Emily to go away.

That wasn't going to happen.

Austin put his arm around her shoulders.

But there was nothing anyone could do right now to make her feel better.

All she wanted was to get her daughter back. But her hope was beginning to fade.

As a car backfired outside, Austin took her elbow. "Come on. Let's get out of here. We don't have any time to waste."

twenty-six

THIS TIME, Austin didn't take the subway.

Larchmont had arranged another vehicle for them.

It should be waiting a couple of blocks away.

Austin's thoughts blurred as he ushered Emily down the sidewalk.

What might Larchmont be hiding? Austin hadn't been able to stop thinking about the possibilities since their phone call. It didn't make sense that Larchmont would keep things from him.

Except maybe it did.

Larchmont had headed up the secret military program Austin and his colleagues had been a part of. The man had been a father figure to many of the guys who were now a part of the Shadow Agency.

But how much did they really know about the

man? Not much. Larchmont didn't share anything about his personal life. In fact, his entire existence seemed to revolve around the agency.

Certainly, there were parts of Larchmont's life that he didn't speak of. Someone didn't get to Larchmont's position without acquiring some skeletons in the closet.

Austin wanted to believe the best of the man, but he'd seen too much and felt too jaded to do that.

In his profession, trusting the wrong people could get him killed.

He did, however, want to send that photo of Bree to Larchmont. Maybe his boss could trace the location where it had been taken. Maybe there was a small detail to indicate where Bree was.

It was worth a shot.

Austin had felt a surge of pride when he'd seen the strength in Bree's gaze. His little girl was a fighter. Maybe she'd even gotten that from him.

But still, she'd be no match for whoever had taken her. She was only six, and these men were ruthless.

Finding her was of the utmost importance.

"What about the stuff we left in the other SUV?" Emily asked as they paused near a silver SUV.

"Don't worry about it," he murmured. "It's not safe to go back to that vehicle. We can buy new clothes for you and makeup and toiletries. Whatever you need."

Austin reached under the wheel well and found a magnetic key box. He unlocked the door for Emily, waited for her to climb inside, and then climbed inside himself.

As he cranked the engine, Emily turned toward him. "I know I've mentioned this before, but I don't have money to pay you right now. I know all of this must cost a lot—"

"I'm not worried about that." He waved her off.

She pressed her lips together before shrugging. "I just don't want to owe anyone anything . . . although for Bree's sake, I will."

"We'll get everything sorted. I mean it when I say don't worry about it. I've got a personal stake in this now too." The words were sincere, and he hoped the emotion came across in his voice.

Emily had enough to worry about without adding finances to it.

She nodded before crossing her arms and settling back in the seat. But she still appeared uneasy, with the tight lines around her eyes and the thin set of her lips.

Austin quickly programmed the address to Peyton's place into the GPS.

He'd already called Trevor. His colleague was going to help.

Right now, Austin just wanted to get out of this city and all the trouble here.

———

AUSTIN TOLD Emily they were going to Peyton's place.

The GPS indicated it was just over two hours from here, depending on traffic, which would only be increasing with rush hour.

Her nerves pulsated at the thought of going to Peyton's place. But she'd do whatever necessary if it meant getting Bree back.

Even if it meant facing the devil himself.

Was that really what she thought about Peyton? In some ways, yes. He was the most self-absorbed, money-hungry person she'd ever met.

If he'd taken Bree . . . then Emily hoped he got the justice he deserved.

He wasn't a good person. He didn't deserve to prosper.

But sometimes, that was the way life worked.

As they moved out of the city, the sky became

darker. More wide-open spaces appeared as the skyscrapers faded and the lots became more spacious.

"So what's our plan once we get there?" Emily's voice sounded strained, even to her own ears.

Austin shrugged. "Initially? I want to see his house."

"And not initially?"

"I need to see if Bree is there. I know you realize this, but every minute counts in situations like this. We're going on forty-eight hours now."

"I know." Emily rubbed her neck as she felt an ache there.

Austin glanced at her. Then he reached across the space between them, took her hand, and squeezed it. Not so much in a romantic way as it was as a means of comfort.

"We're going to find her, Emily," he murmured. "We are."

She nodded, her throat burning at his reassurance.

She'd been doing this single parent thing for the past few years. But really even before that. Paul had never been much of a father.

He'd seemed gung ho about being a family man when they'd first gotten together. Then he'd proven to be short-tempered and impatient. Not exactly father of the year material.

Emily had been relieved whenever he went out of town on business trips because it was more peaceful in the house. She didn't have to walk on eggshells and worry about his moods or what she might say to set him off.

She'd been contemplating a plan of action before Paul's death. Should she talk to him about going to counseling? Would his pride allow him to get therapy? Should she simply suck it up and endure his moods for the rest of her life?

And what about Bree? How did his temperament affect her?

He'd never laid a hand on her—Emily would have left him in an instant if he did. But words could hurt also.

Then he'd been killed when he was in the wrong place at the wrong time. He'd gone into a commercial building he'd purchased to meet with a buyer. The buyer hadn't shown up, but a homeless person had lit a fire inside to stay warm.

Except the fire spread.

Paul had been trapped and . . .

After the fire at her house, Emily could only imagine the horror he'd felt.

There had always been questions about the incident, however. The homeless man had also died in the blaze. But some had questioned if the whole thing was accidental or not.

Part of her had grieved Paul's death. Another part —though she'd never admit it aloud—had been relieved.

She glanced at the GPS again.

They were only ten minutes away.

Only ten minutes from possibly finding answers.

Again, she closed her eyes and prayed for Bree. Prayed for her safety. Prayed for Austin's wisdom and his safety as well.

Then Emily prayed for her own strength to get through this.

Because this situation was testing every part of her faith.

As if to confirm that thought, a message appeared on her screen.

It was Fire Inspector Garnet. He'd left another message.

Her blood went cold as she read the transcribed words.

We need to question you about the fire. I've been talking to the fire inspector in New York, and we've been sharing notes. It's of the utmost importance that we speak.

Her heart pounded harder.

She knew what that meant.

The similarities between the incidents were uncanny.

She was a suspect.

And if Emily didn't find the real culprit, she might be found guilty in both of the incidents.

twenty-seven

INSTEAD OF GOING STRAIGHT to Peyton's house, Austin met Trevor at a nearby hotel.

His colleague had brought gear with him, including some black clothing, bulletproof vests, and comms. They'd need to be extra cautious in this situation, especially considering the fact they didn't know what they were up against.

Trevor had also brought some water, beef jerky, and granola bars.

Emily munched on one of those bars as she paced the hotel room.

Meanwhile, Austin and Trevor had spread a blueprint of Peyton's house on the table to formulate the best way to get inside.

They'd been examining it for ten minutes when Emily paused. "Aren't we wasting time?"

"We need the cover of darkness right now," Austin told her. "I know it seems like time is ticking away, and I know this is difficult. But we don't want to jump in feet first and make things even messier than they already are."

She nodded and pushed her hair behind her ear. Then she started pacing again.

Austin wished she'd get some rest, but he knew that wasn't a possibility. He couldn't blame her. Too much was on the line.

Finally, he and Trevor had their plan.

It was eight o'clock now. They would drive to Peyton's house, park a safe distance away, and go the rest of the way on foot.

He turned to Emily. "We're ready. But I need you to stay here."

Without missing a beat, she shook her head. "I need to go."

He shook his head with equal fervency. "It's not safe."

Her gaze softened until her eyes almost looked pleading. "I'll wait in the car. I promise. The only reason I left the SUV earlier, while we were in the city, was because I knew those men would grab me if I didn't."

Although Austin understood her rationale, he remained hesitant. "You coming with us still doesn't sound like a good idea."

She stepped closer and looked up at him, her eyes definitely pleading now. "Please. If you find Bree, I want to be there when she's rescued. She's going to need me. She'll be terrified."

The sincerity in her words nearly undid him. An ache gripped his heart.

Her words made sense. Austin knew he could trust that Emily would do what she said.

He just worried about other dangers that might find them.

But he wasn't going to talk her out of this. He could see it in her gaze.

Finally, he nodded. "Okay, you can come. But I just need you to know what you're getting into."

———

EMILY'S THOUGHTS RACED. She was so thankful Austin had let her come along.

She sat in the back of the SUV, while Austin and Trevor sat in the front chatting about their game plan.

She'd tried to pay attention at first, but eventually

she tuned them out. It was all over her head anyway. Too many tactical words and military acronyms.

Instead, she prayed for Bree.

In between those prayers, her thoughts shifted to the future. She imagined Bree being rescued. Imagined bringing her home.

But Emily didn't even have a home to return to right now.

She would need to figure out where she and Bree would stay. What life would look like. Where they might move and what kind of career Emily would dive into.

Would she go back to being a psychologist?

She supposed that depended on how things went with Conrad.

Then there was Austin . . .

Emily assumed he'd want to get to know Bree.

Or was that a wrong assumption? Maybe he was perfectly content with this private security thing. Maybe he still didn't want to be tied down.

Should she tell Bree who he was? It only seemed right.

However, Emily had to protect her daughter—including her daughter's heart. She didn't want Bree to meet her father only to be abandoned by him.

Emily and Austin definitely needed to have some serious talks.

Though she sensed something about him was different, she didn't want to make any assumptions.

However, if he *did* want to be a part of Bree's life, then things would be different for all three of them.

Good different? She wasn't sure.

She struggled to make sense of things.

Her gut told her that Austin was a good guy. But did good guys have one-night stands? Yet the fault wasn't all on him either. It was on both of them. Emily had also had a one-night stand. She'd done things she wasn't proud of.

The problems between them were a two-way street.

As Austin pulled the SUV into the woods, Emily's lungs tightened.

This was where the rubber hit the road.

twenty-eight

AUSTIN TOOK one last glance at Emily, hating the fact he had to leave her.

But it was the only choice that made sense. There was no way she could go with him. She'd only be a liability.

Even bringing her this far and having her wait in the SUV came with some risks. What if those men found her again? What if something tragic happened inside, and Austin didn't return?

He didn't want to think about the possibility. But it was only realistic.

He had no idea what would happen once he was inside Peyton's place.

If he didn't make it back, Emily would have to make some tough decisions.

But Austin would do everything in his power to ensure that didn't happen.

He turned to Emily and gave her a nod. "You know the drill."

She swallowed and rubbed her throat, worry filling her gaze. "I do. I stay here. I'll text if anything happens."

"No one should know you're here," he reminded her. "No one should see you."

She nodded again, but her gaze looked unsettled. The emotion made sense. This situation was risky. A lot was on the line.

Nothing could go wrong.

Yet he'd asked her to simply wait and trust him.

She wasn't in an easy position.

But this was the only way.

"We're leaving the keys," Austin told her. "Just in case."

"Got it," Emily told him.

Then he and Trevor climbed out.

First, the two of them would get a lay of the land. The property was secluded, located on ten prime acres and surrounded by a nine-foot-high fence.

As far as Austin knew, there were no guard dogs or other obstacles to stop them from getting close to the house. The most challenging part would be getting inside without being seen.

Thankfully, they were experienced in these things.

He and Trevor scaled the fence and stayed close as they approached the house. They needed to be on the lookout for any security systems or anything else to alert people inside to their presence.

After he'd pulled into the woods and concealed the SUV, he'd noticed a couple of cars coming down the lane. Peyton's place appeared to be the only one down this way.

Maybe Peyton was having some people over.

He and Trevor darted to the side of the house and peered in through a window.

He spotted six men sitting around a poker table, holding cards in one hand and cigars in the other. Glasses with amber-colored liquid sat beside them, and laughter floated toward the window.

"Poker night," he muttered. "Perfect."

From what he'd read, Peyton wasn't married and didn't have any kids. He could have hired help onsite, maybe a housekeeper or someone else. But Austin would guess the bulk of people inside were around that table right now.

Quickly, he and Trevor moved along the exterior

perimeter and peered inside each window. But they didn't see anyone else.

However, simply looking through the windows wasn't going to cut it. They needed to check inside.

Carefully, they walked to an entrance near the garage. Gage, who was helping them remotely, had already hacked into the house's security system. He'd disabled the cameras.

Austin began to pick the lock.

But the tremors returned.

His arms and hands shook so badly that he couldn't hold his tools still.

"You okay, man?" Trevor asked.

Austin swallowed hard, determined to push through. "I'm fine."

"I get those too sometimes."

He stole a glance at his colleague. "Do you?"

He continued to pick the lock.

"It makes me wonder . . ." Trevor muttered.

"Wonder about what?"

"About the side effects of all those experiments they put us through."

Austin's throat tightened. He'd thought the exact same thing.

Finally, he heard a click.

The lock had released.

He turned the knob, and the door opened.

Austin tried to put the conversation out of his mind as he and Trevor stepped inside the house.

———

EVEN THOUGH EMILY knew Austin and Trevor had only been gone for fifteen minutes, it felt like an eternity. She wanted to see what they were seeing. To know what they knew.

Mostly, she wanted to know if Bree was in that house and if she was okay.

She nibbled on her bottom lip as she waited.

Could Peyton really be behind this? That was the question she kept asking herself.

She'd never liked the man. He'd caused a lot of distress in her marriage when he sent her pictures of Paul having dinner with another woman.

He'd wanted Paul to fail—in all things: business, marriage, life in general.

Emily had been taken aback by the photos at first. But Paul had explained the woman he met with was an investor.

Were they actually having an affair?

Emily hadn't thought so.

Though sometimes she wasn't sure. She supposed

it didn't matter anymore. She'd suspected that he hadn't been faithful to her, but she'd never had any real proof other than the photos Peyton had sent.

She knew Peyton had also spread other rumors about Paul in the business world. The man had even gone as far as to hit on her, telling Emily she'd be better off with him.

He'd do anything to get ahead.

Then again, so would Paul.

That made the two of them a toxic combination.

Sending photos of Paul with another woman was one thing. But kidnapping Bree? Would Peyton really take things this far?

She let out a heavy, burdened sigh at the question.

Her thoughts then shifted to Conrad. Emily had been so convinced Conrad was behind this. But Austin wasn't as convinced.

Conrad had honestly seemed to like Bree. Would that have stopped him from putting her through the trauma of a kidnapping?

Maybe.

Then again, Emily still believed the man would do anything to have a relationship with Bree, even if she wasn't his flesh and blood.

The bottom line was that Emily still had no idea what was going on . . . and she hated that fact.

She continued to wait, each second feeling more like an hour.

She couldn't believe this was happening. Kidnappings were something that happened on the news, but not to her or anyone she knew.

Then again, so were one-night stands and accidental pregnancies. Life hadn't exactly turned out the way she'd envisioned. But each step of the process had taught her something new. Had made her stronger. Had made her less judgmental.

There had been a time in her life she'd thought she was above all this. That she'd never find herself in these kinds of situations. That one-night stands and accidental pregnancies were for careless people who didn't have their acts together.

But sometimes all it took was a moment of weakness.

She glanced down at the floorboard and saw a piece of paper.

She picked it up. Turned it around.

It was a photo.

Had it fallen out of Austin's pocket? That was the only thing that made sense.

In the picture, Austin stood with his arm around a beautiful blonde.

Wait . . . was he currently with someone else?

A lump formed in Emily's throat. Why hadn't she considered that? Why hadn't she considered the fact that, not only could he be dating someone, but if he was, that would be one other person in Bree's life?

What if Emily didn't like his girlfriend? What if she wasn't a good person?

Why hadn't Austin given any indications he was in a relationship?

She wasn't sure.

Nor was she sure why the thought bothered her so much.

Yet it seemed like another obstacle to deal with.

And Emily was so tired of dealing with obstacles.

But above all, she just needed to concentrate on getting her daughter back.

She'd figure out the rest later.

twenty-nine

THE HOUSE HAD one main level as well as a room above the garage. Austin had seen nothing suspicious in those areas.

But the massive basement had Austin curious. It seemed the most likely place to hide someone.

Austin had studied the blueprints and knew where the stairway leading to the basement should be. But the entrance was right around the corner from where the men played poker. He'd need to be careful.

As he waited around the corner for the right moment to move, parts of the men's conversation drifted to him.

"I heard through the grapevine that Paul's widow . . ." one man started. "What was her name again?"

"Paul *Rankin's* widow?" another man said. "Emily, I think. My wife used to go to therapy at her practice. She loved the woman."

"I heard the place Emily was renting burned down," the first man said.

"She disappeared off the face of the earth," someone else said. "I wonder what happened."

"Probably wanted to separate herself from those Rankins . . . she must have finally realized they're no good."

"Was she hurt?" a fourth man asked.

"I don't think so. But the police think it's arson. I heard they're looking for her."

"Another arson? Did police suspect the fire that killed Paul could have been arson?"

"I think so."

A pause stretched. "That's suspicious."

Wait . . . Paul had died in a fire?

Why hadn't Emily mentioned that yet?

Austin kept the fact stored in the back of his mind.

He remained close to the wall and carefully opened the basement door. Soundlessly, he slipped inside.

He turned on the small light on his phone to guide him down the stairway.

Then he paused at the bottom.

A large workout room greeted him.

He headed to a door on the other side. Inside, a wine cellar stood, filled from ceiling to floor with various bottles of the liquid.

Then Austin ventured toward the other side of the large room.

He looked inside every door he passed, just in case.

But Bree wasn't inside any of the rooms. Mostly, they were closets and storage.

Then he opened a door across the room, and a hallway appeared.

Who in their right mind needed this much space? This many rooms in a basement? Especially a single man.

But maybe this house was more like a trophy to the man instead of a home. Austin had met the type before. From what he'd heard about Peyton, the man fit the profile.

Austin started down the hallway. The first room was a theater room. Another was a library. The third appeared to be set up for gift wrapping.

Just as he stepped into the last room a footstep sounded behind him.

Austin was certain it wasn't Trevor.

Quickly, he slipped into the room and shut the door.

He waited in the darkness to see if he'd been discovered.

———

THIRTY MINUTES, Emily mused.

That was all the time that had passed.

She'd hoped things might speed up as it got later, but no luck. Everything moved along just as slowly as it had before.

Her phone buzzed.

Her heart leapt into her throat. Maybe it was Austin with an update.

But when she looked at the screen, her heart sank.

It wasn't Austin.

The message had come from the same number as those texts she'd received regarding Bree.

She could hardly breathe as she clicked on it.

The words on the screen made her head spin.

YOU'RE LOOKING **in the wrong direction.**

FEAR PULSED THROUGH HER. Looking in the wrong direction?

How did the sender know what she was doing?

Unless someone was watching her.

Her gaze swerved around the surrounding trees.

Did someone know she was here? Were they watching her without her knowing? Did this mean Austin could be in danger?

If anyone had come near the SUV, she would have noticed.

Right?

Or maybe someone was playing head games with her.

Then another thought hit.

What if Conrad wasn't as noble as Austin thought? What if she and Austin had been set up when they came here?

Quickly, Emily texted Austin. She had to let him know.

What if he was ambushed?

Part of her wanted to jump from the vehicle and run to the house to warn him and Trevor. But she couldn't do that. She'd promised Austin she wouldn't.

Instead, she typed the text message.

Could be a trap. Get out ASAP.

She hit Send.

Then she sank lower in the seat and prayed as she waited for him to respond.

She hoped he got the message before anything terrible happened.

thirty

AUSTIN LISTENED as the footsteps came closer.

It wasn't one set but two.

The men were talking.

"Can't believe that about Emily," one of them said. "It's a shame. She seemed nice enough."

"Too good for those Rankins."

"I wonder who did it. Who set the house on fire? The same person who killed Paul?"

"Maybe."

Austin's heart beat harder.

He'd definitely need to ask Emily about Paul's death.

First, he needed to get out of here.

The doorknob leading into the room turned.

Someone was coming inside.

His phone vibrated in his pocket, but he didn't dare move.

Instead, he remained behind the door and watched as a narrow ray of light cut across the floor and wall. The light illuminated several humidors filled with cigars. There were probably thousands of dollars' worth of Cubans in here.

Illegal Cubans if he had to guess.

"I'll be right there," a man muttered. "I just want to grab some more cigars."

"I'll grab another bottle of whiskey."

Austin listened as one set of footsteps paced away.

Then a man stepped into the room.

Peyton.

Austin braced himself for whatever happened next.

As the man turned toward him, his eyes widened.

He started to yell.

Austin grabbed him before he could and put him into a headlock.

Peyton struggled against him, his elbows flying into Austin's chest and side.

But Austin was trained for this. He held on tight, deciding to wait the man out.

He'd get tired soon.

Finally, the man stilled.

Austin hadn't wanted to knock the man out—he wanted to get some answers. So he made sure he was still conscious.

"Where is she?" Austin demanded.

"Where is *who*?" Peyton's voice sounded strained under the pressure of Austin's arm at his windpipe. "What are you talking about?"

"Bree."

"Who is Bree?"

Irritation pinched Austin's spine. "Paul Rankin's daughter."

"Paul Rankin's daughter? How would I know where she is?"

Austin let out a sigh. "Rumor has it that you kidnapped her."

Peyton froze. Then he let out a barklike chuckle. "Why would I kidnap Paul's daughter?"

"That's what I'm trying to figure out. Maybe as revenge since you hated Paul so much."

"Paul is dead." Peyton tugged at Austin's arm, trying to loosen his grip. "What reason would I have to get revenge now?"

"You tell me."

"None. I have no reason to want to get revenge.

I'm in the real estate business, not human trafficking. I don't hurt people like that. I buy up small, struggling companies. Some people consider it slimy. I see it as a way of helping."

Austin paused and let the man's words sink in.

Just as with Conrad, Austin believed him. Peyton sounded truly surprised.

Besides, Austin had looked all over the house and hadn't seen any evidence that Bree had been here.

So why had Conrad implicated this man?

Austin wasn't sure what was going on here.

He muttered, "I'm sorry to have to do this."

"Do what?"

Then Austin squeezed the man's neck tighter.

Peyton struggled again, elbows and legs flailing. His body thrashed. His hands gripped Austin's arm, trying to release his stranglehold.

Austin added just enough pressure to make the man pass out.

Then he quietly laid him on the floor.

He had to find Trevor and get out of there.

But first he checked his phone.

Saw the words that Emily had texted him. *Could be a trap. Get out ASAP.*

What? Why had she sent that?

Either way, there was no time to waste.

EMILY'S HEART beat so fast she thought she might have a full-fledged panic attack.

A bad feeling lingered in her gut, indicating something horrible was about to happen.

She feared how many people might be hurt.

No matter her feelings about Austin, he was the father of her daughter. Emily didn't want to see anything bad happen to him.

She started to sink lower in her seat when something in the distance caught her eye. She froze just a moment before straightening her neck.

Was that a . . . light?

She had to be seeing things.

Her gaze fixated on the area where she thought she'd seen the illumination.

A moment later, the light appeared again.

It was small and moving, almost bouncing.

A flashlight? Maybe.

Thankfully, the SUV blended in with the trees. Unless those guys shined their lights this direction, no one should see her.

She hoped.

As she continued to watch, a shadowy figure came into view. A man.

He headed toward the house in the distance.

Emily swallowed hard at that realization.

Then another light appeared on the other side of the road.

More than one person was out there.

She squinted, trying to get another look.

Then one guy shined his light on the other.

That was when Emily saw the gun strapped on his back. She didn't know what kind it was, only knew that it looked dangerous.

Deadly.

Those men were headed right toward the house where Austin and Trevor were.

More panic thrummed through her.

She grabbed her phone and texted Austin again. She didn't dare call in case she might give away his location.

Austin and Trevor were already in a precarious situation. But if these two guys with their high-grade military weapons stumbled upon them, things would only get uglier.

She couldn't just sit here and let that happen.

She had to do something. But what?

She scrambled to come up with a plan. She couldn't stop them as she was, with no gun and no training. She'd basically be offering herself as a sacrifice and Austin and Trevor would still be harmed anyway.

But she had to do something!

As her thoughts raced, Emily prayed she'd come up with an answer.

thirty-one

AUSTIN'S PHONE buzzed in his pocket as he hurried down the hallway.

Quickly, he grabbed it and glanced at the screen.

TWO MEN with guns headed toward house. Get out!

WHAT?

Austin's heart raced.

Was Emily safe? He had to get to her. He had to get out of here.

He picked up his pace and met Trevor in the workout room at the bottom of the stairs.

"Emily said there are gunmen outside."

"What?" Trevor asked in a hushed whisper.

"We need to get out of here."

His colleague nodded toward another door. "I had to take that guy out, but he'll be okay."

"Peyton's out too."

Movement sounded at the top of the stairway.

"Peyton?" a deep voice called. "You need help down there?"

Austin and Trevor slipped into the shadows beneath the stairs where they couldn't be seen. Austin gripped his gun, but he'd only use it if absolutely necessary.

They watched as a man slowly walked downstairs, glancing around with every step, before heading toward the humidor.

In only a matter of moments, he would find Peyton passed out on the floor.

Then things would become even more precarious.

As soon as the guy disappeared down the hallway, Austin turned to Trevor. "Let's get out of here. Now."

Wasting no more time, they hurried up the stairs.

Austin paused at the top and made sure no one else was nearby. Voices drifted from the distance—voices that sounded clueless about what was going on.

Instead, they talked about women and business conquests.

With a nod to Trevor, the two of them quietly moved toward the door beside the garage. Without a sound, they opened it and stepped outside.

He held up his arm to stop Trevor from going anywhere.

Instead, they paused.

Listened.

"Did she say where these guys were?" Trevor whispered.

Austin shook his head, still listening.

His hearing . . . it had always been above average. He could hear things before anyone else could. The military had somehow enhanced that.

Right now, the absence of any sounds unnerved him.

He heard the wind. The men laughing behind them. The grass rustling with the breeze.

If Emily was right, those men with guns were coming this way.

But where were they now?

Then he heard the crackle of a radio in the distance.

The next instant, bullets peppered the ground around them.

EMILY HEARD THE GUNFIRE.

Those men . . . they were firing at Austin and Trevor, weren't they? What if Bree was with them?

Here Emily was still sitting pretty. It wasn't right. She wasn't powerless.

Besides . . . Bree was her daughter! She would do anything to protect her.

Then an idea hit her.

She didn't have any weapons or training . . . but she *did* have this SUV. It could be a weapon within itself if she used it the right way.

Her muscles tightened.

One part of her just wanted to hide and pretend this wasn't happening. But she couldn't do that. Not when people's lives were on the line.

She slid into the driver's seat and started the engine. Then she backed out of the hiding space and onto the lane leading to Peyton's house.

She gripped the steering wheel so tightly that her hands ached.

She hesitated just a moment.

Then she sucked in a shaky breath. Stared at the road in front of her. Wasting no more time, she hit the accelerator.

The SUV charged forward. She flipped on the headlights to see where she was going. Who was in front of her. What dangers lay ahead.

Now that she'd started, there was no turning back.

She had to do this. To see it to completion.

She flew down the lane, gravel rumbling beneath the SUV's tires.

More gunfire sounded.

She tried to block out the scenarios forming in her mind. Scenarios where Austin and Trevor were hurt.

Finally, her headlights illuminated two men in black. They stood near the fence with their guns aimed at the yard.

Exterior lights on the house flared to life, and she spotted Austin and Trevor crouching on the lawn.

She searched for Bree's tiny body.

The girl wasn't with them.

Emily bit back her disappointment.

At least Bree wasn't in the line of fire right now.

Still, she had to help Austin and Trevor. There was nowhere for them to run for cover.

They were practically sitting ducks right now.

She didn't take her foot off the accelerator, despite the tremble that rumbled through her along with her adrenaline.

Then one of the gunmen turned.

Raised his gun.

Pointed it at her.

The air left her lungs.

Emily sank lower in her seat, trying to make herself less of a target.

The man fired.

Her windshield shattered, raining pebbles of glass all over her.

She swallowed a scream, her courage wavering a moment.

Whatever she did, she vowed not to slow down.

thirty-two

AUSTIN GRABBED his gun and glanced around.

There was nowhere to hide out here except behind some shrubs, which would offer no protection.

Making matters worse was the fact that the security lights had come on, spotlighting them in the yard.

Commotion sounded inside the house. Yells and shouts.

Would Peyton and his friends call the police?

Then Austin would have to explain why he'd been inside.

Only if he survived long enough to do that.

Just then, headlights flooded the lane.

Austin lifted his head, trying to see what was going on.

Were the police already here? Or did that car belong to one of the gunmen?

He watched as one of the gunmen turned toward the vehicle. Fired at it.

Then he recognized the SUV.

It was his.

Emily was behind the wheel . . .

What was she doing?

Tension gripped him.

He could run to her. Try to help her.

But that would only get him killed.

His eyes widened when he saw Emily charging toward the gunmen.

The next moment, the SUV hit one of the men. He flew in the air before landing with a thud on the ground.

That was what Emily was doing, Austin realized. Using the SUV as a weapon.

Smart thinking, even though her actions could get her killed.

What was she planning on doing now?

The gunman who'd been hit by the SUV shouted obscenities as he writhed on the ground. He cradled his arm as if it were broken.

Austin's gaze shot to the other gunman.

The man stood frozen, almost as if stunned.

Austin and Trevor needed to use this to their advantage.

They exchanged a silent look before darting into the side yard. They needed to stay in the shadows.

They reached the fence without any more gunfire. They scaled it and then remained in the darkness as they headed toward the SUV.

Austin prayed that he could make it to Emily in time.

———

EMILY HAD no idea what she was doing. But she'd come this far, and she wasn't going to back off now.

With one man already on the ground, she carefully backed up the SUV, making sure not to run over the downed man.

Then she set her eyes on the other gunman.

The guy turned toward her. Raised his gun.

He was ready to take her out.

She stayed low as she pressed the accelerator.

More bullets fired.

Her back window shattered.

A bullet lodged into the headrest above her.

But she kept charging forward.

The second gunman disappeared.

She threw on the brakes and glanced around.

Had she hit him?

She couldn't be sure.

She couldn't see anything over the hood of the SUV.

She put the vehicle into Reverse and backed up, hoping to confirm he was out of commission.

But no matter how far she backed up, her headlights illuminated only grass.

The gunman wasn't there.

Her pulse pounded so loudly in her ears she could hardly hear anything else.

Where had he gone?

She *had* hit him, hadn't she?

She'd thought she'd felt an impact.

Maybe she'd just clipped him.

She scanned the area around her again, but she still didn't see him.

He could be anywhere. He could have his sights aimed on her right now.

She pressed on the accelerator and backed up farther.

As she did, she glanced up. Looked for Austin and Trevor.

But they were gone.

Were they on the ground? Had they been hit?

She should have thought this through more. There were so many possible scenarios, and she wasn't sure how each would play out.

She knew one thing for sure. She couldn't leave Austin and Trevor here. She had to figure out where they were.

What if they were injured on the other side of that fence? Should she scale it? Even if she could, it wasn't like she could carry the men to safety.

Her thoughts came to a standstill when movement caught her eye.

The second gunman, she realized with bated breath.

He stood near the tree line.

He must have dived out of the way and then scrambled out of sight.

But, at the moment, it appeared he'd risen from the dead.

He was holding his gun . . . and a red dot appeared on her chest.

If he pulled that trigger, she'd be dead.

thirty-three

AUSTIN STAYED at the edge of the woods, Trevor behind him, as they both tried to remain out of sight.

He'd seen everything that just happened.

Including the gunman who'd dived out of the way of the SUV and hid in the woods.

Did Emily have any idea the man was there?

He didn't think so.

Austin watched, trying to anticipate the man's next move.

His breath caught as the gunman stepped out.

Aimed his gun at Emily.

Even if Emily hit the accelerator, the bullet would pierce her before she could move.

Remaining low, he pulled out his own gun. His

tremors had returned. He got them on occasion, always out of the blue. Sometimes they lasted a few seconds, sometimes a few minutes, sometimes longer.

The important thing was that they always passed.

But he had to do this.

He had to get his shot the first time.

He drew in a breath, trying to calm himself and steady his hands.

There was no time to wait.

He pulled the trigger.

The bullet hit the gunman in the shoulder, and the man collapsed to the ground.

Austin released the breath he'd been holding.

"Let's go!" he shouted.

He and Trevor darted toward the SUV.

Trevor headed toward the driver's seat. Motioned for Emily to get in the back. She scrambled over the console.

Austin jumped in the passenger seat, brushing some glass shards from the seat as he slammed his door shut.

Without wasting any more time, Trevor took off.

"What were you thinking?" Austin called over his shoulder to Emily.

"I was thinking if I didn't do something you guys were going to die."

Her choice had been noble . . . but also stupid. She could have been killed.

Yet another part of Austin admired her bravery. It had taken guts to do what she'd done.

He kept his gun in hand, alert to any danger as they pulled away. He couldn't let down his guard.

Just then, another bullet sliced the air.

"Emily, get down!" he yelled as he slid lower in his seat.

The first gunman must have recovered enough to pull the trigger.

Another gunshot echoed.

The SUV shifted.

Lurched.

One of the tires had been hit.

"We've got to keep going," Austin said.

Driving on the rim wasn't smart, but they had to put distance between themselves and these gunmen. Ruining this SUV was the least of Austin's concerns.

The SUV bounced and jostled down the road.

But they kept moving forward.

Austin kept his gun raised, looking for any other signs of trouble.

Finally, they reached the main road.

The hotel was about a mile away, and Austin thought they could make it there. But they'd need to stash this SUV somewhere out of sight once they arrived.

These gunmen had an unusual knack for finding them, and Austin shouldn't make it any easier for them. Plus, there weren't that many hotels in this area.

These men's ability to track them didn't make sense.

His phone, as well as Emily's, was untraceable. They both had all new clothing. A new vehicle.

So how were they being tracked?

Austin rubbed his neck, which suddenly felt achy and sore.

He needed to talk to Emily.

She would certainly have questions for him. Questions about Bree.

But they'd need to wait until they were in the safety of the hotel room first.

———

EMILY'S entire body quivered as she headed to the hotel room. Trevor had dropped them off and then gone to stash the SUV away somewhere.

Austin kept a hand on her elbow as if afraid she might pass out.

They reached the room, and Austin ushered her inside, led her to the couch, and made sure she sat down.

He carefully lowered himself onto the cushion beside her and studied her face. "Are you okay?"

She nodded, but her body and her brain felt disconnected, as if they weren't working together.

Was she going into shock?

Maybe.

Breathe in and breathe out, Emily. In and out.

She had to get a grip.

After a few more minutes of controlled breathing, she asked, "I assume you didn't find Bree?"

He shook his head, regret lining his eyes. "She wasn't there. Again, there were no signs she'd ever been there."

An ache filled Emily's chest cavity. She'd been so desperate for answers. With every dead end, her hope began to fade.

"But if she's not there . . ." Her voice sounded scratchy.

"We're going to keep looking." He ducked his head low until their gazes met. "Okay?"

Emily forced herself to nod.

Their two best leads had turned out to be nothing.

She licked her lips, determined not to give in to despair. "Who were those men?"

"I'd like to know that also. At first, you thought Conrad had hired them."

She nodded. She'd been convinced that was true. Conrad had made the most sense.

Until he hadn't.

"Could Peyton have hired those guys instead?" She still tried to make sense of things.

"I questioned him, and he seemed clueless, just like Conrad. Besides, if he hired those men, it seems as if his private security would have been inside his gates and not sneaking around outside. Also, there's no evidence of Bree at the house."

Her gaze locked with Austin. "So you think we've been looking in the wrong direction?"

If that was true, then they'd wasted a lot of valuable time.

If it wasn't Peyton or Conrad, then who?

The possibility that a stranger had taken Bree wasn't something Emily even wanted to try to comprehend. It was too terrifying.

"We're going to figure it out." Austin said the words slowly, almost as if he wanted to give her time to soak in his promise. "But, Emily, you could have been killed tonight."

"I know." There was no need to deny it.

Emily pulled out her phone and showed him the text that read: *You're looking in the wrong direction.*

Her gaze locked with his. "Austin . . . I think someone is playing games with us."

thirty-four

AUSTIN APPRECIATED the fact that Trevor had been keeping an eye on the parking lot for the past hour as they waited to see if those men would show up.

But so far, there had been nothing.

However, that text Emily had received left him unsettled.

Had someone been out there watching Emily? Would this person punish Bree because Emily was looking for her daughter?

He prayed that wasn't the case. But there were a lot of uncertainties right now. Most of them, he chose not to voice aloud.

Austin knew Peyton most likely wouldn't call the police. The man wouldn't want law enforcement nosing around on his property—especially with those illegal cigars. Those gunmen would be arrested if they were found out so they wouldn't call the police either.

There was a good chance nothing would come of this.

But if those men had tracked them this far, they could track them to this hotel also.

Which was why Austin and Trevor needed to maintain a lookout.

Gage had been called back to help them. He'd arrived ten minutes ago and had brought some food with him.

They would take shifts keeping an eye on things. They couldn't afford to let down their guard.

For now, Gage and Trevor headed to an adjoining room.

Austin had wanted some time to talk to Emily alone. They had too many unspoken conversations.

The two of them sat on a couch, sandwiches in their laps, and ate. Emily had a turkey and cheese, and Austin an Italian sub. The conversation was fairly generic. Maybe both of their minds needed a break from talking about everything that had happened.

As they finished their sandwiches, he wiped his mouth and took a long sip of his drink.

"Emily . . . I hope you don't mind me asking this, but how did Paul die?"

Her face went pale and her motions grew stiff. "He . . . I know how this is going to sound. He died in a fire."

"A fire like the one at your place?"

She nodded. "I guess. It was suspicious. They said it was accidental, but . . . I always wondered if there was more to it."

Several minutes of silence stretched between them.

Then he turned to Emily.

Something had been pressing on him for a while, something he needed to get off his chest. "Emily . . . I'm sorry."

She glanced over at him and blinked in confusion. "Come again?"

"I'm sorry. For everything."

Her gaze softened then narrowed as she murmured, "It's not your fault we can't find Bree."

"That's not what I mean." His throat burned as regret filled him. "I'm sorry I didn't give you my full name. Or a way to contact me. I'm sorry I left in the middle of the night. I'm sorry I was that guy."

Her cheeks reddened. "I suppose I was that girl also."

"But you weren't. I knew you weren't. I knew you were different—in a good way."

She shrugged, the motion lethargic. "I threw my sensibilities to the wind for one night, trying to see how the other half lives. Other than Bree, it was a huge mistake."

Austin licked his lips, his mouth suddenly dry. Talking about his emotions wasn't something he was good at. Give him a fist fight any day.

However, there were things that needed to be said.

"If I could go back and do things over . . ." he continued.

Emily tilted her head, her voice still soft. "But none of us can do that, can we?"

He shook his head at the truth of her words. "No, we can't."

They exchanged a glance.

As he studied Emily, a tear trickled down her cheek. His heart nearly broke at the sight. She'd been through so much—many of those things alone.

She deserved better.

"I'm so worried about her, Austin," Emily whispered.

The ache in his chest only intensified. What he wouldn't give to fix this.

He *would* fix this.

But it wouldn't be easy.

Sometimes, it felt downright impossible.

Despite his good sense, he reached for her. Pulled her into his arms.

He held her, one grieving parent clinging to another. Each with different circumstances. Austin without a true relationship with Bree yet feeling a bond born by blood.

In his own way, he understood the heartache of this situation.

He stroked Emily's hair as he murmured, "We're going to find her. I promise you that. We're going to find her."

———

EMILY WAS ALL TOO aware of Austin's arms around her. She should probably push him away. Put distance between them.

But she couldn't. She'd been craving comfort and connection.

She'd had no one and had felt so alone for the past two years. For longer than that, to be honest. Even when she was married to Paul, she'd felt a disconnect.

However, right now, she didn't feel alone.

She had Austin.

She reminded herself not to get emotionally attached to this man. Even though he seemed different, there was a good chance he would leave again.

She couldn't handle that a second time.

Plus, she'd seen that photo of him beside that woman. He'd most likely moved on in the years since they'd last seen each other.

Why wouldn't he? He was good-looking and kind. Of course some woman had captured his attention.

Besides, Emily wasn't the same person she'd been seven years ago.

She was older and wiser now with more responsibilities. Logically speaking, she would be fine if she had her heart broken again. But still, she didn't want to put herself through that emotional turmoil again.

Yet as she remembered Austin's apology, her heart softened toward the man. He'd sounded so sincere. His words held so much regret.

She believed him when he said he wished he could do it all over again.

So did she.

But mistakes were a part of life. Some were bigger than others. Some required learning harder lessons.

In the end, it was important for people to allow their mistakes to make them into better humans.

Emily would like to think that was what she'd done.

Become stronger. Better. Tougher. More understanding and less judgmental.

In the future, she'd make more mistakes. Everyone did.

Instead of beating herself up, she would try to learn from those as well.

However, she hoped this moment with Austin wasn't one of those mistakes.

Reluctantly, she pulled out of his arms and used the edge of her sweatshirt to wipe her cheeks.

"Thank you." The words came out as a croak.

Austin stared at her, a strange yet intriguing look in his eyes.

A look that made her heart lodge in her throat.

A look that made her want to fall back into his embrace.

Neither of which were things she should do—especially if he had a girlfriend.

She pointed with her thumb to the bathroom behind her. "I'm going to freshen up. Maybe try to get some sleep. I assume we'll talk about a new plan in the morning?"

He nodded, unreadable emotions lingering in his gaze. "Absolutely."

Before they could talk any more, Emily disappeared into the bathroom. Her emotions overwhelmed her, and she needed some time to sort out her feelings . . . before she did something she regretted.

Again.

thirty-five

AN HOUR LATER, Austin climbed into bed.

Gage was keeping guard outside so the rest of them could get some rest.

Austin was grateful for his support system.

His colleagues, in many ways, had become like family to him.

They'd all been through the same horrors.

The same experiments.

Austin appreciated knowing other people had his back and understood what he'd gone through.

As he lay in bed, he reflected on the hug he'd shared with Emily.

Having her in his arms felt right. Felt natural. Felt like something he wanted to do again and again.

But their relationship—or lack thereof—had been broken from the start. Possibly broken beyond repair.

For that reason, Austin had to remind himself not to get too close.

However, he needed to somehow make things right. The best way to start was by finding Bree.

He turned over in bed and let out a long sigh.

How exactly had they been tracking Emily? He couldn't stop asking himself the question. It just didn't make sense.

If not Peyton or Conrad, then who? And how?

Tomorrow, the team would meet again so they could figure out their next plan of action. As it stood right now, he didn't even have any ideas.

That wasn't okay. But every possibility he considered was a dead end.

He desperately needed a breakthrough. Some insight.

His phone buzzed, and he glanced at the screen.

Larchmont.

He quickly clicked on the text message.

His eyes widened at what he saw there.

Larchmont had researched the metadata on the photo of Bree that had been sent to Emily.

It turned out the photo had been taken in . . . Wyoming.

Wyoming?

That location couldn't be a coincidence.

And, at once, the entire investigation seemed to turn upside down.

———

EMILY COULDN'T SLEEP. Instead, she lay in bed, thinking about how things could have been different.

One or two different decisions, and Bree wouldn't be in this spot right now.

Emily wasn't just thinking only about the one-night stand. She was thinking about everything that happened afterward.

She knew that looking back on a past she couldn't change was unproductive. Still, she gave herself a moment to do so anyway. She needed to sort out her thoughts and emotions. Ignoring her feelings wouldn't do any good.

Reflection was never a bad idea.

She'd known from the moment she met Austin that he was different. That she was attracted to him. That what they shared was more than just physical.

But the timing had been all wrong, hadn't it?

As she stared at the shadowed ceiling, she heard Austin rustle then rise.

She stiffened with curiosity. Where was he going?

She remained frozen and listened. Heard the door open.

Not the exterior door.

The connecting door to Trevor's room.

Austin was going to talk to his colleague . . . in the middle of the night.

Had something happened? Had he remembered something?

She froze, not wanting Austin to know she was awake.

Then she heard voices.

Carefully, she got out of bed. Tiptoed across the room.

Maybe she shouldn't. Maybe listening in was too intrusive.

But what if Austin was sharing something she needed to know? Sharing something that he might not tell her on his own?

In the end, that's why she eavesdropped.

As she stood there, none of the conversation made sense.

Something about Wyoming. Brigitta.

Who was Brigitta? His girlfriend? Was she the woman Emily had seen with Austin in that photo?

Then she heard Bree's name.

This didn't just have to do with Austin's work at the Shadow Agency. This whole conversation somehow still tied in with Bree.

And Emily wanted to know how.

thirty-six

AS A SHADOW FILLED THE ROOM, Austin jerked his gaze up.

Emily stood in the doorway, her arms crossed and hurt in her eyes.

He sucked in a breath. He'd tried not to wake her. But knowing Emily's turmoil, she probably hadn't been asleep at all.

"What's going on?" Her voice sounded hard, almost accusing.

He turned toward her as he stood in the middle of the room with Trevor. "I was trying to let you rest."

"I can rest later," Emily said. "When Bree is safe."

He exchanged a look with Trevor before stepping closer to Emily. "I asked my boss to trace the origins of that picture of Bree that was sent to you."

Her eyes widened. "And?"

"And . . . he was able to track the location on it."

She straightened, a new hope filling her gaze. "Is she somewhere close?"

"No," he quickly said, not wanting to get her hopes up. "The metadata isn't precise enough to nail down an exact location. It just gives a general area."

"So where is she?"

He swallowed hard before saying, "Wyoming."

"Wyoming?" A knot formed on Emily's brow, and she shook her head. "Why in the world would someone take Bree to Wyoming?"

"Why don't you sit down?" Austin said. "You're going to want to as I explain this."

Emily hesitated before sitting on the edge of the bed. Then she waited.

Austin sucked in a deep breath as he contemplated where to start. This was going to be a lot, and he worried about Emily's reaction.

He had no choice but to dive in. "Unfortunately, I've made my fair share of enemies in this job. One of them is a woman named Brigitta Johansson."

"Who is this Brigitta woman?"

"Brigitta Johansson is . . ." He let out another breath. How did he even explain Brigitta? He wished he could forget the woman. "She's pure evil. She's a scientist by trade, and she worked for the Swedish government. In the process, she became friends with others in Europe who shared a similar vision to her own."

"And what vision is that?" Emily's words still sounded stiff and cautious.

"Brigitta doesn't believe that everyone here on earth deserves to live, and she's determined to do something about it. She was working on a drug that could be inhaled and kill people instantly."

"What?" Her voice lilted higher.

Austin wished his words weren't true. "My team heard she was close to completion, and we were ordered to take her out. All the intel was in place. She was living in Turkey at that time—she'd fled Sweden after an arrest warrant was issued for her. She was at home alone when the raid happened." His voice dropped. "Or that's what we thought."

Emily's eyes widened. "What do you mean?"

"We confirmed there was one person inside. But Brigitta . . . well, it wasn't her. It was her . . . it was her daughter."

Emily gasped. "Her daughter?"

Austin nodded stoically as the horrible memories pummeled him. "Brigitta actually had her when she was thirteen, and the two of them looked like sisters."

"How did you accidentally kill her daughter? How did you not know she was in the house?"

He'd asked himself that question a million times also. "Honestly? I believe Brigitta knew something was coming and planted her daughter at the house, knowing the two looked alike and we would be confused."

Emily's hand flew over her mouth to cover the O of horror. "She would do that to her own daughter?"

"She's heartless—and I don't say that lightly. I mean it. Apparently, she and her daughter hadn't been seeing eye to eye. Maybe Brigitta thought we'd take her alive. Or maybe Brigitta secretly wanted to get rid of her."

"That's terrible."

"When we found out Brigitta survived, we knew we were in trouble," Austin said. "The good news was that we destroyed her lab and the experiments she was doing there. But she knew we were responsible for the attack."

"We?"

"Me and my team," Austin explained. "Me even more specifically. She created a video and posted it online, a video where she vowed to retaliate. However, she's been in hiding since then. She's on every agency's most wanted list."

"Did she stay in Turkey?"

"We've heard rumors she managed to slip into the US."

"And if she came here . . ." Emily's voice trailed.

"It would be to exact revenge."

"So you think that this woman who hates you took Bree?" Emily asked the question slowly as if still trying to comprehend the situation.

Austin shrugged before nodding. There was no need to hide the truth. Besides, Emily would see right through him. "It's the only thing that makes sense."

Emily shook her head, a touch of disbelief still in her gaze. "How would she even know Bree is your daughter? I didn't even know your last name."

His gaze darkened. "Clearly, someone else knows I have a daughter. That's why that man gave you the name of the Shadow Agency after the fire. He knew if you called the agency, somehow I would put the pieces together."

"Your boss is the only one who makes sense, right? Is he working with this Brigitta woman?"

Austin reeled. He'd never considered the possibility that Larchmont might be working with Brigitta. He couldn't imagine Larchmont taking things that far.

Yet, on the other hand, Emily had a point. There

was a connection he was missing. Someone who wasn't being forthright.

Austin had been easy on Larchmont so far. He'd tried to respect him as a boss.

But now he needed more answers.

Emily looked him dead in the eye, her lips parted in what appeared to be disbelief. "Let me get this straight. What you're telling me is that Bree's kidnapping is about you?"

Her words felt like a slap in the face.

But Austin had no choice but to nod. "Unfortunately, I now believe that's correct."

———

EMILY RUMINATED on Austin's words.

She hadn't seen this one coming.

Hadn't thought for a moment that revenge against Austin could be the motive behind Bree's kidnapping.

It certainly sounded like he'd made his fair share of enemies in his line of work. But why would anyone take Bree?

Unless someone—this Brigitta woman—wanted to teach him a lesson.

If Brigitta blamed Austin for killing her daughter,

then maybe she wanted to make Austin feel that same pain.

Emily rubbed her throat, which suddenly felt tight. Too tight. Like she couldn't get a breath.

She forced herself to swallow before turning back to Austin. "So what does all of this mean? How do we move forward?"

Austin's gaze was unwavering, as if his mind had been made up. "We go to Wyoming. We track Brigitta down. When we do, we'll find Bree."

He sounded sure of himself, like this was what they should do. But Emily still had questions and concerns. So much still didn't make sense.

"Do you think this woman will hurt her?" she asked.

Emily watched Austin's expression, determined to see the truth in his gaze. The last thing she wanted was for him to lie to her. She needed to know how precarious this situation was.

"I think Brigitta mostly wants to hurt me," Austin said. "Luring me to Wyoming is most likely her end goal."

Emily tried to think that through, tried to follow his line of reasoning. Did all the puzzle pieces fit?

She wasn't sure.

She turned to him again. "So those men that have been following us . . . you think Brigitta hired them?"

Austin nodded stiffly as he sat on the edge of the bed. "It makes sense. She has a lot of money and resources. I wouldn't put it past her."

"So why try to kill *me*?" How did that fit into all of this? That fire was meant to be the end of her. How would that hurt Austin?

"That's a good question," Austin said. "I'm not sure."

Finally, Emily nodded and rose. "Okay then. Wyoming it is."

"I don't think it's a good idea that you go." Austin twisted his head doubtfully as he pulled his lips into a tight line.

"It's like I told you earlier—when we find Bree, I want to be there for her. You're not going to be able to keep me away. Try whatever you want, but I'm going with you."

A moment of quiet passed before he said, "It's going to be dangerous."

"Then let it be dangerous. I'd walk through fire for my daughter."

In fact, she'd tried to do exactly that when her house had gone up in flames.

Austin didn't even bother to argue.

thirty-seven

THE NEXT MORNING, Gage drove them to a small executive airport where they would board a private plane for Wyoming. Larchmont arranged a flight for the four of them, which was helpful considering there was no way Emily could get a plane ticket without her ID.

Part of Austin wished he could leave Emily here in New York, but he knew that wasn't a possibility.

He was surprised they hadn't had any more trouble since last night. He expected those guys to show up at the motel to try and finish what they'd started.

But they hadn't.

Why? Somehow those men had been able to track them. So why stop now?

Granted, one of them had been shot and another hit by Emily in the SUV. But Austin knew there were at least four men. What about the other two?

Perhaps the biggest question on his mind was how Brigitta knew about Bree. It made no sense. And it bothered him.

If Emily didn't even know his last name, then there was no paper trail to follow that would have led Brigitta to him. Yet somehow, it appeared she'd found out.

They were mostly quiet on the drive. He sensed Emily was nervous. He couldn't blame her.

Finally, they pulled up to the airport. Trevor and Gage hurried inside to meet the pilot.

Austin took a minute to speak with Emily. "You ready for this?"

She didn't hesitate before nodding. "I'm ready to get my daughter back."

Silence passed a moment, and his thoughts swirled. A new question hit him. "What do you think Bree will think about me?"

Surprise flashed in her gaze. She hadn't expected that question, had she? Nor had he expected to ask it. But the thought had slipped out.

"I think . . . I think that you're going to be her hero."

Something about the words caused warmth to rush through him.

It solidified even more his need to find Bree. To get to know her. To have a relationship with her.

But Brigitta . . . she wasn't someone to be messed with. He frowned as he remembered the woman with her wacked-out ideas and determination to do anything—and hurt anyone—to get what she wanted.

And she hated Austin.

That would make this even more complicated.

Austin rolled his shoulders back and climbed out of the car.

He'd defeated her once. He would do it again.

ONCE SHE WAS SETTLED in the airplane, Emily couldn't stop thinking about Austin's question. At first, she hadn't known how to answer it.

Then she decided to go with the truth. Bree would think Austin was a hero—and not just because he'd rescued her from this situation. But because the man had a larger-than-life vibe to him.

Bree was going to think Austin hung the moon.

If things had been different, Emily might have

thought the same. Austin had so much potential—if he could only get past his demons.

He'd come a long way in the seven years since she'd seen him.

A moment later, they taxied down the runway and lifted into the air. Once the turbulence calmed down, she released her breath. Something about taking off and landing always made her tense. She'd heard those were the riskiest times of flying.

She glanced at Austin. His arm shook as it rested on the armrest.

The sight took her by surprise, and concern filled her.

Without thinking, she grabbed his hand and squeezed. "Does flying make you nervous too?"

He didn't pull away. "No. I just get tremors sometimes."

Her eyebrows knit together. "Tremors?"

He shrugged. "It's not a big deal."

"Sounds like a big deal. How long have you been getting them?"

Austin shrugged again, clearly uncomfortable with the conversation. "For a while."

"Have you seen a doctor?"

"Saw one of Larchmont's guys." He paused. "Said it was just some nerve damage. I could take medicine for it, but I didn't like the side effects. So I decided just to live with it instead."

Emily continued to study him, realizing there was still so much she didn't know about him.

She'd learned the night they met that he wasn't close to his family. That he'd pretty much left home right after high school and hadn't gone back.

That he'd joined the military.

That he'd undergone some special training.

She knew his instincts were quick. His intellect sharp. His sense of hearing phenomenal.

He seemed to know how to react in every situation. How to defend himself. She'd even heard him on the night they met speaking fluent Swedish to a tourist.

What kind of person could randomly speak Swedish, of all languages?

"What did you do in the military?" Emily pulled her hand away, realizing she'd been holding his for too long.

Austin did a double take at her. "What?"

"What did you do in the military? Were you special forces?"

He stared out the window before shrugging. "Not officially."

"What does that mean?"

He glanced around as if her question set him on edge.

Whatever he did, it was top secret, wasn't it?

"My friends and I did the jobs that nobody else wanted to do," he finally said. "Jobs where it was best to remain unattached."

The reality of his words hit her. Emily knew exactly what he was saying.

That was why he'd been the way he had all those years ago. He couldn't get tied down. Making connections could be the difference between life or death.

All those facts had made him into the person he was today.

The military had practically trained him to be a lone ranger.

But what a terrible life that must be. Sure, Austin had his colleagues. But they didn't replace the bonds and connection of a family.

His colleagues wouldn't take care of him one day when he was old and unable to do so for himself. His colleagues wouldn't throw him birthday parties or give him hugs to relieve the stress of a hard day.

Emily mentally shook her head and snapped from her thoughts. Why was she feeling sorry for the man? He'd disappeared when she was pregnant with his child.

But again, she reminded herself that wasn't all his fault. She'd played a role in all that.

Plus, she wanted to understand him.

Despite her determination, her resolve to keep her distance from him began to soften.

She often told her clients that behind every bad behavior was a hurt from the past.

That was true for her.

And it was true for Austin.

thirty-eight

AS AUSTIN SAT on the plane, he wished he could share more with Emily. That he could pour out every-thing about his past to someone.

But that *definitely* wasn't smiled upon, and his colleagues were entirely too close. Not that they should make a difference.

He didn't want to do things in secret. But some-times he thought it would be nice to have someone other than his colleagues to talk to. To share the things he'd been through. The things he'd done.

To have an intimate bond with someone.

But it was better if he didn't wish for something he couldn't have. Better if he simply accepted his fate.

He was destined to be a nomad. To do jobs that

required him to remain unattached. To go through life virtually alone.

But now Bree was in the picture. That was a fact he'd have to contend with and figure out how to handle.

There was no way he was walking away from his daughter. He'd vowed he would be different than his own dad. He'd be present and loving and work hard to have a good relationship with his children, to offer them a safe place to call home.

He rested for the remainder of the flight. He'd need his energy once they landed.

Finally, Alan Larchmont's ranch came into view below.

It had been a while since Austin had been here.

He also knew this was the area of Wyoming where Brigitta was supposedly hiding out. That was the intel he'd received from his colleagues.

No doubt she'd moved here with a purpose—probably to taunt the Shadow Agency.

They didn't have proof yet that she was definitively here. But everything pointed to that theory being correct.

All this time, he'd hoped and prayed that the person who took Bree wouldn't hurt her. That they just wanted something from Emily.

But now that he knew Brigitta might be responsible . . . all those hopes went out the window.

He had to find his little girl and rescue her. There was no other option.

A bell chimed above him.

It was time to prepare for landing . . . and to prepare for finding Bree.

———

EMILY DIDN'T REFUSE when Austin slipped his fleece-lined jean jacket over her shoulders after they deplaned in Wyoming. It was much cooler here than it had been back in New York, especially with the wind whipping down over the mountains.

As Trevor and Gage chatted with the pilot a few minutes, she paused beside Austin on the airstrip.

She glanced at the towering mountains in the distance. Beside her stood a sprawling house with two barns behind it and a creek rippling to the east.

The area was absolutely breathtaking.

Austin followed her gaze.

"I've always wanted to come out here," she told him. "It's even more beautiful than I thought it would be."

"It is gorgeous, isn't it?"

"Absolutely," she said. "You come here a lot?"

"A few times a year. This property is owned by my boss, Alan Larchmont. He invites the team out here for retreats or to get some R&R on occasion."

"Seems like the perfect place to do that."

"Maybe when this is all over, I can show you some of my favorite spots."

Her cheeks warmed.

Then she reminded herself of that picture she'd seen of Austin with that woman. Maybe she should ask him about it. But this just didn't seem like the time.

Maybe when all this was over she would. But for now, she should keep her distance, despite her growing feelings.

If Austin had a girlfriend, he was off-limits.

Austin seemed to sense the change in her and nodded toward the house. "Let's get inside. I know we don't have any time to waste. I heard Larchmont cooked some brisket and potatoes for us. So let's grab a bite to eat. We're going to need it in order to keep our energy up for whatever the rest of this day holds."

Emily nodded, ignoring the ripple of nerves rushing through her.

This was the day of reckoning.

She followed Austin toward the house, her desperate prayers coming more fervently than ever.

thirty-nine

LARCHMONT WAITED at the door for Austin, Emily, Trevor, and Gage as they approached.

Larchmont with his six-foot-five thin but muscular frame. His salt-and-pepper hair. His tan skin. His well-deserved wrinkles. The man's motions were precise, his words carefully chosen, and his mind always seemed to be calculating something.

He'd never said his age, but Austin would guess him to be in his late sixties.

Austin let Emily step inside first and introduced her to Larchmont. Recognition flashed in her gaze.

Larchmont was the one who'd given her that card from the Shadow Agency, wasn't he?

Then again, Austin had guessed that from the start —he just hadn't known why.

His house was sprawling and magnificent. Austin always told himself if he ever came into a great amount of money, he'd buy a place like this in an area like this.

It was a slice of heaven on earth.

While Larchmont's assistant ushered them to the table, Austin turned to Larchmont. "Can I have a word?"

"Of course. Excuse us." Larchmont nodded down the hallway, and together they walked toward his office.

Austin felt Emily's gaze trailing him, but he didn't offer any explanation. Not yet. He wanted some answers first.

Once the door was closed, Austin turned to Larchmont, his muscles bristled. "You knew, didn't you?"

Larchmont stared at him, blinking as if clueless. "Knew what?"

"Don't play dumb. You knew I had a daughter."

Larchmont's face showed no reaction.

That was all the answer Austin needed.

Fire raced through his veins. "Why wouldn't you tell me something like this?"

Larchmont sat in one of the leather chairs in his office. He motioned for Austin to sit in another on the other side of his desk, but Austin had no desire to sit. He was too wound-up.

"Fine." Larchmont shuttered his eyelids the way he

did when annoyed. "Have it your way. Emily came to the base asking if anyone could identify you."

"How did you even know about her?"

"I keep an eye on all my men. Your personal lives . . . well, they aren't personal. I told everyone at the base to say they didn't recognize you."

"Why?" The question came out as a bark.

"I didn't want you to be distracted from the jobs you were doing."

Tension continued to mount inside him. "Did you know Emily was pregnant?"

Larchmont shrugged. "Not right away."

"But you did know . . . you knew I had a daughter and didn't tell me!"

He lowered his eyelids a moment. "Part of me did regret it. But if you were always thinking about a child you had back at home, then you wouldn't have been focusing on the job I needed you to do."

"There was no room for a personal life doing that line of work, huh?"

"I told you that from the start."

Austin couldn't deny those words. Larchmont had told him that. "I deserved to know."

Larchmont nodded stoically. "Maybe you did. But I had to make an executive decision. The work you did for our country was important."

"More important than my child? I might as well have been a mindless robot."

"But you aren't a robot," Larchmont reminded him. "This country wouldn't be the country it is today if it wasn't for the work you and the rest of your colleagues have done. You made great sacrifices. You still do. I wish you could get the recognition you deserve for that."

"It should have been my choice!" Austin's hands fisted.

Larchmont's eyes widened for a moment, but he nodded. "You're right. It should have been. There were things I should have done differently. But, unfortunately, that's all water under the bridge now."

Austin wasn't so sure about that.

"How did Brigitta find out?" Austin watched his boss carefully, determined to learn the truth.

Something flickered in Larchmont's gaze. "That I can't tell you. You'll have to ask her yourself."

Finally, Austin sat down. "I need you to tell me how I can find her."

———

EMILY TRIED NOT to be impatient. Tried to eat. To engage in the conversation around her, which seemed entirely too lighthearted.

But none of those things happened.

She wanted to know what Austin and Larchmont were talking about. It was all she could think about.

Was their conversation about Bree?

Most likely.

Did Larchmont have information on where she was? Would he share with Austin?

There were still so many unknowns.

Gage excused himself to take a call from their pilot, leaving Trevor and Emily alone at the table.

Trevor glanced at her and shifted in his seat, something clearly on his mind. "I know he's made some mistakes, but he's one of the good guys."

"What?" His words startled her. "Are you talking about Austin?"

He shrugged and nodded. "Of course. I know you guys have some type of history. But it's not easy to integrate into regular society after everything we've been through."

What did that mean? What exactly had they been through? And what kind of person referred to normal, average everyday citizens as 'regular society'?

Not people Emily knew.

"The situation between Austin and me is . . ." She licked her lips. "Complicated, to say the least."

"I can see that." He paused. "We're going to get your daughter."

"Why do you sound so serious when you say that? Don't get me wrong. I know getting my daughter back is serious. But there's something different about your tone—something that makes me nervous."

"The woman who grabbed her . . . she developed a virus that could have wiped out at least 30 percent of civilization as we know it. She believed it was natural selection."

Emily gasped. "That's horrible."

"She thinks the earth needs to be purified," Trevor continued.

"She sounds like Hitler."

"She could have been a new Hitler. But thanks to Austin, that didn't happen."

Emily let that thought settle a moment. "You weren't a part of that team?"

Trevor shrugged. "I came in a year later. But the stories I've heard about what those guys did . . . it's better than anything you'd ever watch in a movie."

Understanding began to dawn on Emily. A clearer picture of what Austin had been through formed in her mind.

Before she and Trevor could talk more, Gage wandered back into the room. Austin and Larchmont followed.

Emily's gaze lingered on Austin. After talking with Trevor, she saw him in a different light. More understanding rolled over her, and she knew they needed more conversations to talk things out.

Later.

There was no time for those talks now.

However, she couldn't help but think that maybe she'd been wrong about him.

forty

AS THEY ALL sat at the table, they formulated what they would do next.

The intel Larchmont had received was that Brigitta had escaped Europe and had spent some time in Russia for a while before coming to Wyoming.

Austin had no idea how she'd gotten into the country. But there were indications that sometime within the past month, she'd done exactly that. The FBI and Homeland Security had been searching for her, but she'd managed to slip under the radar.

What exactly she was doing here in the US remained a mystery.

But Austin had an idea.

Brigitta had come here to find him. She wanted to punish the man who'd ruined her life.

He had gone undercover to find out information on her, so the woman knew his face. She held him personally responsible.

According to Larchmont, her location was about an hour from here. Austin had no doubt it would be heavily guarded.

But if that was where Bree was, then that was where he'd go.

They finished discussing their plan. Then Austin turned to everyone. "We need to get ready."

They all nodded in agreement. Trevor and Gage would be going with him. Austin knew he couldn't do this alone.

Meanwhile, Larchmont would stay and run the operation from the ranch.

As he turned to Emily, questions lingered in her gaze. He dreaded this conversation. Dreaded what he needed to do.

"Can we talk a moment?" he asked.

She nodded.

He led her into a library and closed the door behind them.

Austin knew she wanted to go with him. Knew that she felt she deserved to go.

Maybe she did.

But Emily going was a terrible idea.

Her earlier words filled his mind. *When we find Bree, I want to be there for her. You're not going to be able to keep me away. Try whatever you want, but I'm going with you.*

He knew she'd meant those words.

He drew in a long breath. "I'm going to go and bring Bree back."

"I hope she's okay . . ." Emily's voice quivered.

"I think she is. I know there's a lot that still doesn't make sense. But I think Brigitta is really after me." He pulled something from his pocket and showed it to her.

She blanched in surprise. "That's Brigitta?"

Surprise rushed through him. That wasn't the response he'd expected. "Have you seen her?"

"I saw that photo. I thought . . ."

He glanced at the picture. "You thought she was my girlfriend?"

"I mean, you look chummy."

"I had to get to know her. It's part of the reason she hates me so much now. She feels like I stabbed her in the back."

Emily shook her head and ran a hand through her hair. "Wow. I just assumed . . ."

She'd thought they were together? No wonder she'd get close only to pull away.

"We can talk about this more later."

"Yes, of course." Emily rubbed her throat again before lowering her voice. "Thank you for all you've done. I'd like to talk more about this later. But right now, we need to get going. I can't wait a minute longer!"

Austin's muscles tightened with dread.

He nodded and took a step back. "Yes, *I* do need to get going."

Then, before Emily could argue, he stepped through the doorway, closed the door, and twisted the lock on the other side. Yes, there was a lock on the outside of the door.

Larchmont had clearly had to use this tactic before. Austin didn't want to think about why.

"Wait . . ." Emily instantly banged on the door. "Austin! What are you doing? Austin!"

"You can't go with me," he said through the door. "I'm sorry, Emily, but this is the only way."

"You've got to be kidding me! I should be there!"

"If you go, you could be killed. Bree needs a mom when this is all over. I can't let you die."

"Austin! You can't do this."

"I'll make it up to you. I'll be back soon. With Bree."

Before they could argue anymore, Austin forced himself to walk away.

He prayed he was doing the right thing . . . and that Emily would forgive him.

———

EMILY BANGED ON the door another moment before finally stopping and pressing her forehead into the wood.

She couldn't believe Austin had done this, that he'd taken things to this extreme.

Of *course* she should be there. She didn't care how dangerous it was. This was her daughter!

She slid onto the floor and pulled her knees to her chest. More tears flowed down her cheeks. She hadn't even realized it was possible for her to cry this much.

But she hated feeling helpless. Hated the fact she couldn't protect her daughter.

Hated . . . well, everything about this situation.

She glanced around, looking for something that might help her.

But the only thing in this room were books.

Books that wouldn't do her much good now—unless there were some on how to get out of a locked room.

She frowned.

How long would Austin leave her in here? What if he didn't return? Was Larchmont gone also? The plan had been for him to stay. But what if something changed?

What if they were all killed, and she was trapped in here with no way out?

Would she die in here?

Her thoughts began to spiral out of control, and she practiced her breathing exercises.

Panic would only handicap her right now. She had to keep her anxiety under control and maintain a cool head.

There was one thing Austin was right about: Emily *had* to stay alive . . . because Bree needed her mom when this was all done.

forty-one

GUILT STILL POUNDED AT AUSTIN.

He wished there had been another way to get out of the house without Emily. But there hadn't been, and he didn't have any time to waste arguing with her about it.

He was mostly quiet, lost in his thoughts, on the drive out to Brigitta's place.

He couldn't help but feel like he was on the cusp of change.

Knowing about Bree . . . it made him want to change.

It made him want more.

And being around Emily . . . it made him wonder what his future would look like with her.

The thought was probably crazy.

Yet it gave him hope—and even more determination to bring Bree home.

"You going to be okay to do this?" Gage's voice pulled him from his thoughts.

Austin nodded. "Of course."

"There's a difference when you have a personal stake in things."

"You have Nia in your life now," Austin reminded him. "Has that changed things?"

Gage had met Nia down in Miami a couple of months ago. Now Gage visited her as often as possible. His friend seemed truly happy.

"Most definitely," Gage said. "I love being with her."

"You think Emily will forgive me for this?" Austin asked.

"I've seen the way she looks at you," Trevor said. "If you bring her little girl back to her, I have no doubt she will."

His jaw tightened. If only this assignment was easy. But it might be their hardest one yet.

"I don't know what this mission is going to hold for us," he told his colleagues.

"We've got your back, no matter what," Trevor said.

Gage agreed.

He knew his friends' words were true. They depended on each other to stay alive. Trust was everything.

But for a moment, Austin felt as if he was bringing a sword to a gunfight.

Knowing Brigitta, she would throw everything into making sure Austin paid for what he'd done. He prayed they were prepared for whatever lay ahead.

———

EMILY WASN'T sure how long she'd been sitting in this room, but it felt like forever. The minutes just kept ticking past.

She'd already searched the room, looking for a means of escape.

There was nothing.

She had no choice but to sit here and wait.

She would never forgive Austin for this. She didn't care how he justified what he'd done.

It wasn't acceptable.

She'd been a fool to ever think that maybe they had a chance together.

Then she heard the lock on the door click.

She rushed to her feet, ready to bulldoze her way out of the room at the first chance.

As the door opened, Larchmont stood there.

Emily lunged at him.

The man caught her arms and locked her in place. "I know you're upset, but calm down."

"Don't tell me to calm down." The man clearly didn't know how to speak to women. His words were practically a death wish. "How dare you let Austin do this?"

He remained undisturbed. "I told him to do this. It was for your own good. He doesn't want you to get hurt."

Emily knew there was truth in his words, but she couldn't bring herself to acknowledge it aloud.

"If you stop acting like you want to hurt me, I'll let you go." Larchmont stared at her another moment. "Is it a deal?"

She imagined all the things she'd like to do, but she knew she didn't have it in her.

Instead, she took in a deep breath and nodded. "Okay. I promise."

Larchmont slowly released her from his grip and stepped back. Emily forced her shoulders to relax. Forced herself to suck in a deep breath. Forced herself to remain calm.

She stared at him, determined to get to the truth of this matter. "Who are you?"

"I run the Shadow Agency. I'm a bit of a father figure to this group."

Fire continued to flame inside her. She didn't like this man. "A father doesn't withhold the blessings from his children."

He raised his eyebrows. "Touché. But relationships are complicated. You're better off staying away from Austin."

The truth of what he was saying hit her, and Emily swung her head back and forth. "You still don't want him getting close to anyone, even though he's not in the military anymore. Does that mean none of your men have any type of relationships outside the Shadow Agency?"

His gaze darkened. "One does."

"You didn't stop him?"

"I thought about it. But it's a new relationship. The woman he's involved with . . . she could be an asset to us."

"So she benefits you?" Emily shook her head in disbelief of this man's selfishness.

An emotionless expression remained in his eyes. "I'm just trying to look out for Austin's best interests. If you're smart, that's what you'll do too. Once your daughter is rescued, you should forget that Austin ever existed."

His words echoed in her ears.

Forget Austin ever existed? Did Larchmont really mean that?

Looking at his serious expression, Emily knew he did.

Even worse . . . what if he was right?

Before her thoughts could linger on the questions any longer, her phone buzzed.

Her breath caught.

Was it Austin with an update?

But as she glanced at the screen, a picture appeared.

A picture of Bree.

The words below the image made her blood go cold.

I HOPE you're playing by the rules—for your daughter's sake.

forty-two

AUSTIN, Gage, and Trevor approached the sprawling house that was all clean lines, gray siding, and black trim. Stylish and expensive—which fit Brigitta.

Trevor pulled out his lock picks and was about to start when Austin twisted the handle.

It easily turned, and the door opened.

He exchanged a look with his colleagues.

Was this door unlocked because they were in the middle of nowhere?

He doubted it. Brigitta wasn't the type to be trusting, especially since she was a fugitive in the United States.

More likely, this door had been left open for them.

Maybe Brigitta wanted them to find her. Maybe she was just waiting for them.

If that was the case, they would need to be even more careful.

Inside, Austin motioned for Gage and Trevor to split up. They went separate ways to search the house.

But the place was strangely absent of life inside—or any signs that life had recently taken place here. The trash cans were empty. No food was in the fridge. No scents lingered in the air.

There were no cars out front or in the garage.

The place appeared empty.

Where was Brigitta? Did they have this all wrong? Had she ever been here in the first place?

Austin's gut twisted.

He and his colleagues met back in a large living area and each confirmed Austin's thoughts. No one was here.

Austin rubbed his chin. "So did Larchmont get bad intel?"

Gage shrugged. "It's a possibility. But he's usually more on top of things than that."

If Bree wasn't here, then where? This had been their next best lead, and he didn't want to let this go.

They were missing something.

Had Brigitta been here and cleared out? Had she caught wind that she might be discovered?

Just as the thought filled his mind, he glanced up.

Something frosty blasted from the ceiling vents, almost like cool air coming from the AC on a hot day.

But it definitely wasn't hot enough right now in Wyoming for the AC.

"What's that . . . ?" Trevor looked up and squinted.

Then the truth hit Austin.

"We've got to get out of here!" he yelled. "Now!"

He already felt the substance from the vents filling his lungs. His eyes burned, and his head spun.

What was it?

Knowing Brigitta, the substance was deadly.

"Hold your breath!" he shouted.

He reached the door and tugged on it.

It was locked.

What . . . ?

Trevor ran to a window and tried to shove it open.

It was locked. Not just locked—it was purposefully sealed shut.

Austin raised his gun. Fired at the window.

But the bullet didn't break it.

The glass was bulletproof, he realized.

He glanced around.

They had to figure out another way to get out of here.

His head swam even more. He needed oxygen before he passed out.

Trevor and Gage also looked disoriented, with clouded gazes and staggered steps.

They didn't have much longer to get out before . . .

He didn't want to finish that thought.

Austin ran to the other side of the room, desperate to find another exit.

Before he reached it, spots appeared in his gaze. His lungs felt like they might burst. The room spun around him.

He dropped to the floor as everything around him went black.

———

AUSTIN OPENED HIS EYES. Blinked. Opened them again. Blinked again.

He lay on a cold tile floor, his cheek pressed against it. Everything was white and bright around him.

At once, everything that happened slammed back into his mind.

Some kind of gas had been released into the room. They'd been trapped. Had passed out.

At least they weren't dead. He'd feared the gas was lethal.

But where were Gage and Trevor now?

Austin tried to sit up, but he couldn't move his arms.

His hands were bound behind his back, he realized.

Despite that, he forced himself upright. A jabbing pain shot through his head. He squinted, trying to remember any more details. But his mind was blank.

He licked his dry lips. His bottom lip was split and bloody. The skin felt tender around his eye.

Had he been beaten?

Based on his aches and pains, he'd say yes.

While Austin had been unable to defend himself, Brigitta must have had her men beat him.

He should be surprised, but he wasn't. The depths the woman would sink to had no limits.

An empty room surrounded him, one that almost looked like a high-tech interrogation room. A door with a small pane of glass at the top stood in front of him, heavy-duty locks near the knob.

Austin didn't have to test the door to know it would be impossible to open.

"I thought you'd never wake up," a voice said behind him.

His muscles tightened as he slowly turned.

Sitting in a simple folding chair against the wall

behind him was Brigitta Johansson. Brigitta with her pale skin, blonde hair, and icy expression.

She looked as if the two of them were having a casual, everyday conversation as she perched with her legs crossed and a faint smile on her face.

"Where is Bree?" he demanded. He moved too suddenly, and the ache pulsed through his head again.

Brigitta flicked her hand in the air. "It's not important."

Austin's hands fisted, and he imagined himself throttling the woman. He needed to get these restraints off.

But he held himself together.

For now.

"What do you want from me?" he asked through clenched teeth.

Brigitta's smile returned, even wider this time. "Everything, my dear. I want everything."

forty-three

EMILY PACED LARCHMONT'S OFFICE, unable to settle down. Not with so much on the line. Not with so few answers.

Larchmont sat behind his desk, looking as cool as a cucumber with his hands steepled in front of him and an expression absent of emotion.

She could hardly stand how calm he was.

"Have you heard anything yet?" she rushed.

"The answer is the same now as when you asked thirty minutes ago." An edge of irritation laced his voice. "No, I haven't heard from them."

"It's been three hours since they left."

"These things take time."

She paced some more. "I know, but I would think you would've heard something by now. You said it would take an hour to get to Brigitta's hideout, so they've had two hours since they arrived."

His gaze darkened. The man clearly didn't like being questioned.

"They're the best of the best," he told her. "If Bree is there they'll find her."

"But what if Bree isn't there?" Emily knew she was annoying the man, but she didn't care. She needed answers—answers that he had.

She wanted to light a fire under him. Get him moving.

She wanted him to feel the same urgency she did.

Instead, he acted as if this was just another day in the office.

"Then we'll have to go from there." His jaw tightened again. "That's what you do in situations like these. You explore Possibility A. If it doesn't work out, you move on to Possibility B. It's the way things work."

Emily wasn't sure if the man was patronizing her or not, but he was *definitely* getting under her skin.

She finally stopped pacing, stood in front of him, and crossed her arms.

She studied Larchmont. He wasn't like anyone she'd ever met before. As a psychologist, she spent a lot of time examining the human psyche.

But Larchmont was different. Powerful. Secretive. Cool under pressure.

Willing to do whatever was necessary to get the job done.

During covert missions, she imagined he was exactly the kind of leader the government needed.

But that didn't make him a good person or role model or father figure.

"I disagree with you." She wasn't willing to let the subject drop.

He raised his eyebrows as if her words had surprised him. "What do you mean?"

"You taught these men they couldn't do their job and have a life outside their career. I believe a person can have both love and duty to their country. Those two things can coexist. It doesn't have to be one or the other."

Larchmont didn't say anything, only offered a quick nod of acknowledgement.

"It's almost like you want to control them," Emily continued, studying Larchmont's face for a reaction.

Just as before, he showed nothing. No doubt he was an expert in interrogation tactics. He knew how to keep his poker face.

"You clearly don't understand what it's like to be in the military," he finally said. "I have to know I can trust them. That they have each other's back. That they're going to listen to orders. If you want to call that controlling them then you feel free."

"They have the ability to follow orders while still having free will, especially when it comes to their time outside work." She wasn't going to let this man get under her skin. "Have you ever considered that maybe they would be even better at their jobs if they had families to come home to? Someone who's there for them no matter what?"

His cheek flickered—though just barely.

She was annoying him, wasn't she? He knew there was truth in her words.

"I appreciate the fact that you're thinking about their best interests," Larchmont finally said. "But why don't you let me be the one who does that? It's what I get paid to do."

Emily ignored his statement and started to pace again. There was no need to argue with this man. She was stuck out here in the middle of nowhere with him.

He was clearly the one calling the shots. And he was arrogant enough not to see his shortcomings.

She glanced at the time again. "How much longer can they go without checking in before you send backup?"

A frown flickered across his lips before quickly

disappearing. "Another hour."

Emily pressed her eyes closed.

Another hour?

She wasn't sure if she could wait that long.

Because she hated not knowing what was going on, and an hour could mean the difference between life or death.

———

"I HAVE BEEN WAITING for over five years to have this conversation with you." Brigitta smirked, her accented words truncated.

"That's because you've been like a rat, hiding out and afraid to show your face—and for a good reason." Austin glowered at the woman.

She chuckled before shaking her head. "You always had spunk, Austin. Part of me admires that."

He ignored her statement. "I don't know why you pulled Bree into this. I'm the one you want. Why don't you let my friends go? They can take Bree, and then you can do whatever you want to with me."

"If only it was that easy." She clucked her tongue with fake compassion. "But it's not. You do realize how greatly you made me suffer, don't you?"

"You wanted to take out a third of the world's

population," he reminded her. "I don't think you have any room to talk."

"I wanted to do it for the greater good. The earth has too many people. It's overrun. We're going to run out of resources. And let's face it—some people don't deserve to be here. They don't pull their weight."

"Now you're starting to sound like Thanos from *The Avengers*." Austin almost wanted to roll his eyes.

Brigitta shrugged, unoffended. "He had a point. How much longer can we sustain ourselves at the current rate we're going? This is simply survival of the fittest. There's nothing wrong with that."

"*Everything* is wrong with that." Austin paused. "I'm sorry about your daughter. She was never supposed to be in that house. But you knew that, didn't you? You traded places with her."

"You took away the one person I loved." Brigitta's cool facade disappeared as fire filled her gaze.

"You wanted us to think you were inside."

"I never imagined you would bomb the building!" Her nostrils flared. "Someone has to pay for what happened! That person is you. The best way I can make *you* pay is by making *your daughter* pay."

Austin's blood turned to ice at the thought of his little girl suffering. "You need to leave Bree out of this. She's just an innocent girl."

"So was my daughter!"

"Your daughter helped you experiment on people with the new drugs you were developing," he reminded her. "She killed twenty people in the process—and she was prepared to kill more. She wasn't innocent in all this."

Brigitta's gaze darkened. "You don't know anything!"

Austin drew in a deep breath. He should have known better than to get Brigitta worked up. She already wanted to harm him.

If he was dead, he couldn't help Bree.

He swallowed hard before asking, "Where are my friends?"

Her gaze darkened. "You don't need to worry about them. You just need to worry about yourself. You thought those experiments the military did on you were bad? You haven't seen anything yet."

Brigitta reached into a small bag beside her and pulled something out.

Austin's eyes widened when he saw it was . . . a blow torch.

"Do you know what my daughter felt when she burned to death?" Her eyes sparkled. "You're about to find out."

forty-four

ANOTHER HOUR PASSED while Emily continued pacing. "I think they're in trouble."

This time, instead of denying her words, uncertainty passed through Larchmont's gaze.

He was getting worried too, wasn't he? Emily could read it all over his face.

She paused in front of his desk, desperate to get his attention. "Can't you send someone to help them?"

"I can. But it will take at least three hours for anyone to get here. There's no one else close. I'm kind of in the middle of nowhere, in case you haven't noticed. I thought for sure the three of them would be able to handle this. They know what they're doing."

"Even people who know what they're doing can be

thrown off course by the unexpected. Maybe that's what happened."

"Maybe." A stormy expression crossed his gaze before disappearing behind a more guarded look. "They should have checked in by now. I sent a text to all three of them about twenty minutes ago, but none of them have responded."

Emily's heart pounded harder. His words only confirmed her fears.

Something bad had happened.

"If you don't have any other men available then you and I need to go," Emily said.

Larchmont's eyes widened, and he let out a puff of air. "That sounds like a terrible idea."

"I know I'm not trained. I know you think of me as a liability in a situation like this. But Bree is my daughter, and I'd do anything for her. I'm good at following orders, and you seem to like giving instructions. Maybe we'd be a good team."

Larchmont silently stared at her for several seconds before letting out a chuckle. "You are pretty convincing. It's a good thing I insisted Austin leave you here."

Emily narrowed her gaze, ignoring the reminder. "I'm assuming you have some type of tactical background?"

The expression on his face almost made him appear offended. "Of course."

She straightened. "Great. Then you'll know what to do."

"Even though I've been out of the field for many years, I'd like to think I still have some of my skills."

"Then what are we waiting for? Brigitta's place is an hour away. If we're going to help them, we need to go now. There's no time to waste."

————

"YOU DON'T WANT to do that," Austin muttered, unable to pull his gaze away from the fire flaring from the blowtorch in Brigitta's hands.

"But I do." She smiled again, her wicked-looking grin proving she was soulless.

She stepped close enough that Austin could feel the heat on his cheek.

His throat tightened.

He tugged at the binds around his wrists, desperate to loosen them.

"I've dreamed about this day for a long time," she murmured with saccharine sweetness. "Now it's here. My dreams can come true."

"Where's Bree?" he demanded, ignoring the sweat

that had begun to pour down his forehead. "And how did you know she was my daughter?"

She waved the torch closer, the fire singeing his bicep. The heat scorched his skin, and the scent of burning flesh filled his nostrils.

The pain became excruciating.

But he gritted his teeth, keeping his expression neutral. He wouldn't give Brigitta the satisfaction of hearing him cry out.

"I started learning everything I could about your past." She shrugged as she paced in front of him. "Doing my research, of course."

His skin still burned, but she didn't step any closer. Didn't try to burn him again. Not yet.

"You always were good at research," he muttered.

Usually Brigitta's research involved the best ways to hurt people and bring destruction.

Brigitta shrugged again, still staring at the flame. "I heard through the grapevine that a woman showed up at the bases asking about you."

"How in the world did you find that out?" Did she have inside sources who were a part of the US military? It wouldn't surprise him—but it did disgust him.

He continued to twist his wrists. He could feel the ropes around them loosening.

"I have sources." Satisfaction gleamed in her eyes.

"Anyway, I kept searching and discovered this woman had a child. I did the math. Looked up the child's picture. Saw the resemblance. And I knew. Then I knew exactly how I should make you pay."

She lifted the blowtorch in the air and watched the flame with a gleeful look in her eyes.

Austin couldn't sit here anymore.

Wasting no more time, he swung his leg. His foot hit the blowtorch.

It cut off and clanked to the floor.

Brigitta turned toward him with startled eyes that quickly filled with darkness.

Austin wrapped his legs around her ankles and jerked.

She tumbled to the floor.

Using all his strength, he ripped through the remaining ropes at his wrists.

Then he jumped from the chair.

But before he could make another move, Brigitta reached into her bag and pulled out a gun.

Her nostrils flared as she said, "Not so fast, Mr. Greenwich. Not so fast."

forty-five

EMILY AND LARCHMONT were mostly quiet on the drive to Brigitta's place. She didn't like the man and had no desire to engage in small talk.

He did run over a few logistical details they'd need to keep in mind once they arrived. But Emily knew she'd be at Larchmont's mercy. She had no idea what she was doing, only that she had to help.

She had convinced him to call the FBI. They were on their way, but at least an hour or two out from the secluded location.

Darkness had fallen outside, and Emily hoped the shadows might prove useful to them.

Larchmont parked down the lane from Brigitta's place, near the SUV the men had driven. "We go the rest of the way on foot."

She nodded. She'd figured that much.

Everything was surprisingly quiet as they approached the ultra-modern house in front of them.

Who even owned this place? Why had Brigitta picked this location specifically?

As if Larchmont was reading her thoughts, he said, "I heard Brigitta paid someone to build this place to her specifications. She didn't do it under her own name because she knew she'd be caught."

That meant she had multiple people working for her. Emily wasn't surprised, but she did store that information in the back of her mind.

"Why did she choose to build here, so close to you?" Emily asked.

"I suspect she did it on purpose, that she wanted to be close when she exacted her revenge."

Emily's thoughts still raced. So much still didn't make sense. "How do *you* know about Brigitta's location here and not the FBI or Homeland Security?"

"One of my guys was able to locate Brigitta a few months ago," Larchmont explained. "I had him keep an eye on her. I wanted to know what she was up to. To my surprise, he was able to follow her into the country. She paid off someone at the border to get in. This house, however, was already built."

"You didn't think to tell anyone she was in the country?"

His gaze remained hooded "I was waiting for the right time. I knew she was here for a reason, and I wanted to know why."

Emily supposed that made sense. But it seemed like someone in Larchmont's position would know—under the orders of those above him—that he should report her presence. Wasn't that what he'd taught his men? So why didn't the rules apply to him?

Maybe because he wasn't in the military anymore.

She didn't have time to think everything through right now.

Staying low, Larchmont gripped his gun as they hurried to the front door.

Larchmont twisted the doorknob, and it gave way.

The door opened.

A sterile-looking living room greeted them. Everything inside was white or gray, reminding Emily of a museum.

Nothing seemed to be disturbed.

Yet she had the strange sense that something bad had happened here. Something terrible even. A faint smell—almost medicinal—lingered in the air.

"Stay behind me," Larchmont told her.

Staying near the wall, they crept through the living room.

Emily's gaze wandered over everything around her. The black iron railings surrounding the second story. The kitchen and dining room just within eyesight. The winding marble stairway.

But still no movement.

If Emily hadn't seen the SUV outside, she might not even think that Austin, Trevor, and Gage were here.

But they must be.

The bad feeling continued to grow.

Something wasn't right.

What had happened once the guys arrived here?

Movement caught the corner of her eye.

She touched Larchmont's arm and pointed.

When she did, the first bullet flew.

———

AUSTIN HEARD THE GUNFIRE.

Had backup come? Had that been Trevor or Gage firing? Or had they been shot?

His heart pounded harder.

As Brigitta stared him down, gun in hand, Austin had no choice but to remain still.

She was too far away for him to take the gun from her. He'd tried to creep closer, but she'd warned him to stop.

He had no doubt Brigitta would pull that trigger if he forced her hand.

But she wouldn't kill him on the spot. That would be too easy.

She wanted him to suffer. The burn mark on his arm served as a reminder.

"Kick the blow torch to me," she instructed.

Austin glanced down. Saw the apparatus on the ground. Remembered the sting of the flame on his flesh. Felt the blisters that had already formed.

He knew exactly what would happen if he gave it back.

He couldn't let Brigitta get hold of it again. Next time, she would make him suffer even more.

"You won't have time to use it," he told her, nodding toward the blowtorch. "Someone else is in the house. Backup. They're going to take you down—just like we took you down before."

Her eyes narrowed. "No one is going to get to you or take me down!"

"I wouldn't be so sure. We should talk. If we strike the right deal, maybe I can convince my people not to kill you."

She stared at him, her eyes still narrow, and her breaths becoming shallower. "How do you know those gunshots weren't from *my* guys? How do you know they didn't take *your* guys down? You Americans are always so arrogant."

Austin shrugged, knowing that she was playing mind games with him. "I just know."

She raised her gun higher. "Then maybe I should just end you now."

His muscles stiffened.

Austin knew he was cornered and at this woman's mercy.

And he had no idea what might happen next.

forty-six

EMILY WATCHED as Larchmont stood in place. In three shots, he took down the three gunmen.

Each of them dropped to the floor.

Her pulse beat in a quick, erratic rhythm in her chest.

Impressive . . . she hadn't been sure Larchmont had such skills. He'd proven her wrong.

Quickly, he took the men's guns and used zip ties to secure their wrists and ankles.

As he did that, she glanced around. "Where's everyone else?"

"This way." Larchmont nodded toward the kitchen.

Inside, he opened a pantry door.

Why in the world was he going into the pantry?

Was he planning on locking her inside, just like Austin had done in the library?

Emily hesitated.

As if reading her thoughts, Larchmont scoffed before saying, "I'm not going to lock you in here. Trust me."

She really didn't trust this man.

She watched as he pressed a shelf at the back of it, and a door opened.

Her lips parted in surprise. "What? How did you know this was here?"

"I didn't know it was here until I studied those blueprints," Larchmont said. "This wasn't on the original design, so I decided to dive deeper."

When had he done that? Why hadn't he shared that information earlier?

A shiver raked through Emily as she followed him down some stairs.

As soon as they stepped into the basement, lights flickered on, buzzing above them. They must be motion-censored.

A central room stretched in front of them. White walls, ceiling, floors. No personal effects whatsoever.

Six doors stood closed around the room.

To her left, another smaller hallway stretched into the unknown.

"What is this place?" she murmured.

"Good question."

Was this where Bree was held? Had Brigitta taken her girl and put her down here?

Emily shivered again, hating to think about everything her daughter had been through. She prayed Bree was unharmed and healthy.

Larchmont opened the door to the first room. A laboratory stared back at them. The next room contained computers and a security system. The next was an office.

On the other side of the space were three empty rooms with white walls and cold gray tiles on the floor.

Almost like . . . exam rooms?

Was that what they were?

Or were they interrogation rooms?

She shivered.

Just being down here left her feeling shaken and cold.

Larchmont started down the smaller hallway and opened the first door.

Then he froze.

A voice drifted into the hallway. "One more step, and I'll shoot him."

Emily's breath caught and she peered around the corner.

A woman stood there, a gun in hand. The pistol was aimed at Austin, whose bloodied and bruised face stared back at her.

Austin . . .

A gasp escaped before she could stop it.

What had he been through?

And the woman . . . she was the one from the picture.

———

AUSTIN RAISED his hands in the air, trying to keep everyone's emotions down.

Larchmont was here.

He sucked in a breath when he saw someone behind Larchmont.

Emily.

Why had she come? Though part of him was happy to see her, she might end up getting herself killed.

"You didn't think I was going to let him escape, did you? That I would let any of you escape?" Brigitta shook her head, her gun still trained on Austin.

"I already took out your men upstairs," Larchmont told her, still holding his gun. "You're not going to walk away from this."

"I beg to differ." Brigitta smirked. "Everything is going to go exactly as I say, or people will die. Including your daughter." Brigitta cast a glance at Austin, clearly wanting to see his expression.

Austin's heart pounded harder.

So Bree *was* here.

But where?

"Just give them Bree and do whatever you want to with me," Austin said.

"Austin . . ." Emily's voice cracked.

He knew that wasn't what she wanted to hear. But it was the truth. He'd do anything to make things right and protect those he cared about.

He hadn't met Bree, but he already cared about her.

And, in his own way, he'd never stopped caring about Emily. It was crazy. They hardly knew each other.

But he knew enough.

He wanted to make things right. He wanted to be the man he should be. To forget about Larchmont's rules. To forget about his training that had basically amounted to brainwashing.

He needed to choose his future.

He wanted that future with Emily and Bree.

But, first, he had to get everyone out of here alive —including himself.

He glanced at Larchmont, wondering if his boss had a plan. The expression on his face was intense but unreadable.

Austin had always known the man was smart. But was he smart enough to get them out of this situation? Austin had never even seen the man in the field.

"You should have stayed out of this," Brigitta muttered.

Who was she talking to? Austin? Or Larchmont?

"We won't let you get away with whatever you're planning," Larchmont muttered.

"He's not going to be happy with this."

He's not going to be happy? Had she misspoken? What did that even mean?

"You need to tell us more," Austin growled.

"Tell you more? More about what?" Her words seemed to curl with satisfaction. "I have so much I could share."

Why did he have a feeling this wasn't about Bree?

"Enough of these games!" Larchmont yelled. "Where's the girl?"

Brigitta's eyes glimmered, and she quicky turned.

Aimed her gun at Austin.

Then a bullet blasted through the air.

forty-seven

EMILY GASPED, the gunfire ringing in her ears.

Had Austin been shot?

She held her breath. Waited for the aftermath. Prayed she was wrong. That Austin was okay.

Then Brigitta crumpled to the floor.

Blood spread from her chest onto the tile around her.

Larchmont had shot Brigitta, Emily realized.

She released her breath as relief washed through her. Austin was okay.

Austin reached for the woman and put his finger to her neck. "She has a pulse but barely. Brigitta." He patted her cheeks. "Where is Bree? Where did you leave her?"

Her eyes popped open. She stared at Austin, almost like she wanted to say something.

But Emily couldn't make out her words.

"Where is she?" Austin asked louder.

"You're . . ." Brigitta rasped.

"I'm what?"

"You're . . . a piece of the . . ."

A knot formed on Austin's forehead. "A piece? What does that mean? Where's Bree?"

"Not . . . done." Then Brigitta's eyes closed, and she slipped into unconsciousness.

"I had to do it," Larchmont put his gun away and stepped closer, his voice void of emotion. "She was about to kill you."

"She needed to tell us where Bree was first!" Austin stood, his entire body bristled as he stared down his commander. "You shouldn't have done that."

"It was either that or she'd kill you."

"She wasn't about to kill me!" Austin's nostrils flared. "She was still taunting us. You knew that."

Emily swallowed hard, trying to keep her cool in the situation.

Austin had some good points. But this wasn't the time to argue.

"You guys . . . finish that later. We have to find

Bree." Her voice shook as she reminded them of the situation. "Where are Gage and Trevor?"

"They have to be around here somewhere," Austin said. "You didn't see them?"

"No, but we didn't have a chance to search all the rooms either."

"We need to start searching."

"I'll go with you," Emily said.

Austin nodded stiffly, casting another dirty look toward Larchmont.

"I'll check this side of the house." Larchmont pointed behind him.

Wasting no more time, they began to search the basement. Each door they opened only led to an empty room.

"I've got Trevor and Gage!" Larchmont suddenly yelled from a distance. "They're okay!"

A flash of relief swept through her before disappearing.

That still didn't tell Emily where Bree might be.

What if her daughter wasn't here?

And what if the only person who knew where Bree was now lay nearly dead on the floor?

———

AUSTIN'S THOUGHTS RACED.

Where could Bree be? They'd searched this whole house.

If only Larchmont hadn't pulled the trigger when he did. Then maybe Brigitta would have told them.

Had Larchmont pulled the trigger when he did for reasons other than saving Austin? Was Brigitta about to say something Larchmont didn't want them to know?

Anger simmered inside Austin at the thought.

But this wasn't the time to deal with it.

Right now, he needed to concentrate on finding Bree.

"Where do you think she could be?" Emily looked up at him, fragile hope brimming her gaze.

This was a pivotal moment.

If they didn't find Bree now, there was a good chance they wouldn't find her at all.

There were no other options. No other avenues to explore or places to look.

Everything hinged on what happened right now.

Austin didn't want to let her down. He wanted to find Bree more than anything.

So what were they missing?

He glanced around the space.

Just then, Trevor and Gage returned from upstairs,

battered and bruised but otherwise fine. The grim look on their faces indicated they hadn't found her up there either.

They hadn't come this far to be set back like this.

Austin tried to put himself in Brigitta's shoes. What would he have done in this situation? Where would he have stashed the girl?

He didn't know.

"Austin?" Emily's voice called him again.

He turned to her, his thoughts still roiling. She was a psychologist. She got into people's heads for a living.

If anyone could dive into Brigitta's mindset, it was Emily.

"I know this is going to sound weird, but Emily, what would you do if you had been Brigitta? Where would you have stashed Bree?"

Her eyes fluttered with surprise as she seemed to realize what he was asking.

Then she closed her eyes as if deeply concentrating.

When she opened her eyes again, an idea lingered there.

Austin held his breath as he waited to hear what it was.

forty-eight

"SHE HAD THIS PLACE DESIGNED, RIGHT?" Emily glanced around, her gaze showing she was still trying to compute something, to confirm a theory.

"That's right," Austin told her.

"Brigitta would want Bree somewhere out of sight." Emily tapped her lips with her finger. She grabbed her phone and found the picture of Bree that had been sent to her. She studied it a moment, moving closer so Austin could see.

"There in the corner." She pointed. "It almost looks like a mirror."

"It does. What are you getting at?" Austin stared at her, waiting to hear the rest.

"One of those rooms Larchmont and I searched . . . it had a large mirror in it."

Austin's eyes lit. "Let's go check it out."

They raced back into the room. Sure enough, a floor length mirror stretched on one wall—a mirror with a weird sheen to it.

Emily held her breath as she watched Austin use the back of his gun to break the mirror.

As the mirror shattered, a room appeared on the other side.

A room with a bed and some stuffed animals.

"Bree?" Emily's heart pounded harder. "Are you in there?"

"Mommy?" Bree peered around the corner.

Emily sucked in a deep breath as relief swept through her.

"Bree!" The next instant, Emily flew into the room and swept her little girl into her arms.

She held her tight until she finally forced herself to pull away.

She examined Bree. Made sure she wasn't hurt.

Her initial sweep didn't show any injuries.

Emily pushed a hair behind her daughter's ear as emotions clogged her throat. "Are you okay, sweetie?"

Bree nodded. "I'm bored. I've missed you. I've just been watching TV."

Emily saw the TV in the corner.

There was some water. Some apples and oranges. Even a bathroom.

How did they even get her in this place?

Then she saw the bookcase.

There must be a hidden door there, just like in the pantry.

Based on what Emily had seen of the basement, she would guess that doorway led into the laboratory. There had been shelves in that room also.

Bree threw her arms around Emily again, and Emily picked her daughter up, still hugging her.

If Emily had her way, she'd never let her little girl go. If only that were possible.

She felt Austin's gaze on them.

A new emotion filled his eyes.

He was seeing his daughter for the first time.

Emily would have to figure out how to break the news to Bree that Austin was her father.

But for now, all that mattered was that her little girl was safe.

———

TWO HOURS LATER, the FBI was on the scene.

Everyone had been questioned. Brigitta had been taken to the hospital. Her men had been arrested. The house had been inspected for any more hidden dangers.

Things finally felt safe . . . except for some lingering questions Austin had for Larchmont.

He also couldn't figure out how those men had tracked him so easily. There was something he was missing.

He rubbed his neck again, feeling an ache there.

Did the ability to pinpoint his location have something to do with the experiments that had been done to him?

It seemed like a good possibility, something he had wondered about before.

He'd address any of those issues later.

For now, he wanted to enjoy this happy moment.

Austin couldn't take his eyes off Emily and Bree. They sat on the couch in the living room, blankets around them and water bottles in hand. The mother and daughter spoke in low tones to each other.

Bree.

His daughter.

The girl was beautiful.

An unusual quiver of nerves fluttered inside him as he tried to think of what to say. He hardly ever got nervous.

But right now, his nerves bounced all over the place.

Shoving his hands into his pockets, he strode toward them, trying to think of a way to strike up conversation.

But he didn't have to.

"Are you Superman?" Bree stared at him.

Austin's eyes widened as he sat beside them. "Superman?"

She nodded. "That's who you looked like when you burst into that room to save me."

A smile feathered across his lips. "Unfortunately, I'm not Superman."

"You look like him to me." Bree shrugged casually, well-spoken for a six-year-old. At least, in Austin's experience, it seemed that way.

His grin widened. "Well, I'll take that as a compliment."

"What's your name?" Bree continued to study him.

"Austin."

"I'm Bree."

"That's what I heard. It's a pleasure to meet you, Bree."

"Do you know my mom?" Bree glanced up at Emily.

Austin looked at Emily and saw a soft smile tugging at her lips.

"As a matter of fact, I do," he said.

"She's the best mom in the whole world," Bree continued.

"I can see that. She wasn't going to stop at anything to find you, you know."

Bree gave her mom another hug. Emily held her close.

"Mom," Bree whispered. "Can he come over and eat with us sometime? I can make my strawberry cupcakes with the sprinkles on top."

Emily exchanged a smile with him. "I think we might be able to arrange that."

Two beautiful females.

Females whose lives Austin would love to be a part of.

But he didn't want to rush anything.

Even though he and Emily hadn't said a word, they both seemed to be on the same page.

Bree would need some time to recover from this. They shouldn't throw too much onto her at once.

But based on the conversation he'd just had with the girl, Austin felt a touch of hope stirring inside him. Maybe he wasn't destined to be alone after all.

epilogue

TWO WEEKS HAD PASSED since Brigitta had been arrested.

Emily and Bree had remained at Larchmont's ranch as they recovered. Besides, they didn't have anywhere else to go. Not right now.

Austin had told her he was based out of Michigan, but he traveled all over and wasn't in one place for very long.

For now, he'd stayed at the ranch also.

He and Bree had been getting to know each other.

Three days ago, Emily had told Bree that Austin was her father. She'd held her breath as she waited for her daughter's reaction.

To her delight, Bree was thrilled to have a superhero as a dad—just as Emily had hoped she'd react.

The father and daughter had been as thick as thieves since then.

Emily hadn't been sure how she'd feel about their new relationship. But, in truth, she loved seeing them together. They already had a bond, and Austin was really good with her. He liked to fly her around the room. To pretend to be a horse and give her rides. He'd even let her braid his hair into tiny dreads.

Eventually, she and Austin were going to have to talk about the future. She and Bree couldn't stay in Wyoming forever. Austin would need to get back to work.

But they hadn't had a good opportunity to chat.

Until now.

Bree had lain down to take a nap. While she slept, Emily stepped outside to get some fresh air and look at the beautiful snowcapped mountains rising in the distance.

Austin stepped out behind her, a smile feathering across his lips. "Hey."

Her pulse quickened. "Hey."

Every time Emily saw him, she had that reaction. She felt that rush of attraction.

They'd gone through a lot together.

Austin had carried that photo of him with Brigitta

in order to remember all that was at stake. To remind him of the impact of his work.

But now, he would carry a picture of Bree.

His daughter reminded him of what was important now.

"I figured we needed to talk," Austin paused beside her.

They weren't touching.

Yet Emily felt as if they were.

She shoved her hands into the pockets of her coat. "That's probably a good idea. I think Bree really likes you."

"I like her too."

"The fire inspector called. He confirmed it was arson, and he also said that the FBI is going to take over the investigation. Since it involves a terrorist, this case moved higher up the chain."

"The good news is that they don't appear to be looking at you as a suspect."

"Yes, that is good news."

Austin sucked in a deep breath before changing the subject. "I've talked to Larchmont . . . and I'd like to take six months or so off from the job so I can get to know Bree. If that's okay with you?"

Warmth spread through her chest. "Of course. That sounds like a great idea."

He let out a long breath. "I guess I'm tired of chasing shadows."

"What do you mean?"

"I mean, I exist as a shadow. As someone whose background has been erased. As someone who's affiliation with the military will be denied. And my missions involve those who hide in the shadows to do their evil deeds. I'm ready . . . well, I guess I'm ready to live in the light for a while."

Emily grinned. "I like that. The light is a good place to be."

He returned her smile. "I think so too."

"Where will you live?"

"I guess that will depend on where you end up."

She nibbled on her bottom lip. "I keep trying to figure that out. My license to practice is in New York. Part of me doesn't want to go back there—although I have talked to Conrad, and I've agreed he can see Bree again. I'm trying to be more open-minded."

Austin turned toward her fully, his total attention on the conversation. "Larchmont is heading back to Michigan soon. He said we could stay here for a while until we get things figured out. What do you think about that idea?"

Emily studied his face. "Do you trust Larchmont?"

His cheek twitched. "Good question. Honestly? I

still think he's hiding something. But I don't know what."

"I'm sure with a job like his that he has a lot of secrets."

"Yes, I'm sure he does. I need to keep all those things in mind when dealing with him. But I don't think he wants any harm to come to me."

Emily nodded. "I'd agree."

Austin stepped closer and lowered his voice. "Emily . . . I'd like to do things right this time."

She paused, unsure about his words. "What do you mean?"

"I mean, I'd like for you to go out with me. I'd like to get to know you better. I'd like to start over, if possible." He paused and swallowed as his gaze probed hers. "What do you think about that idea?"

A grin spread across her face. She didn't even have to think about her response. "I love that idea."

"So, Emily." He paused and cleared his throat. "Would you go on a date with me?"

He looked so nervous, it was touching.

"Hmm . . ." She tapped her finger against her lips. "Intriguing idea. Can I think about it?"

"Really?" Surprise laced his voice. "I mean, sure. If that's what you need."

"I'm teasing. Of course I'll go on a date with you."

A grin spread across his face. "Perfect. I'm not sure what there is to do around here. Or if there are any good babysitters."

"I'd prefer to bring Bree with us, if that's okay."

"I love that idea."

Relief washed through her.

As she stared up at Austin, she felt that flutter again.

She hoped they might have a future together.

A future as a couple, and as a family.

And a future with any other surprises that might come along the way.

~~~

Thanks so much for reading **Shadow Chaser.** If you enjoyed this book, please consider leaving a review.

Coming next: **Shadow Assignment.**
~~~

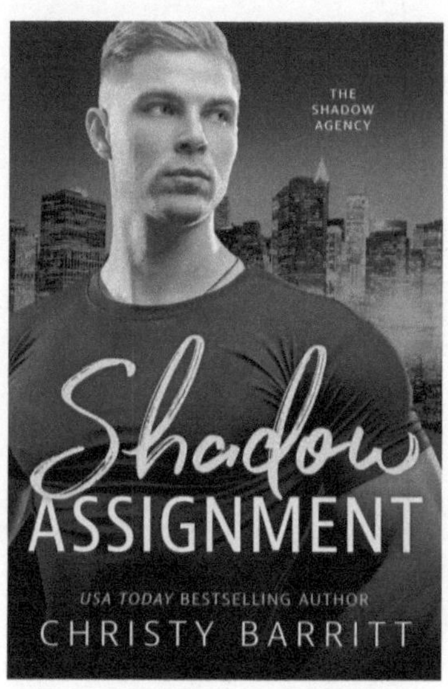
THE
SHADOW
AGENCY

Shadow
ASSIGNMENT

USA TODAY BESTSELLING AUTHOR
CHRISTY BARRITT

about the author

USA Today has called Christy Barritt's books "scary, funny, passionate, and quirky."

Christy writes both mystery and romantic suspense novels that are clean with underlying messages of faith. Her books have sold more than four million copies and have won the Daphne du Maurier Award for Excellence in Suspense and Mystery, have been twice nominated for the Romantic Times Reviewers' Choice Award, and have finaled for both a Carol Award and Foreword Magazine's Book of the Year.

She is married to her Prince Charming, a man who thinks she's hilarious—but only when she's not trying to be. Christy is a self-proclaimed klutz, an avid music lover who's known for spontaneously bursting into song, and a road trip aficionado.

When she's not working or spending time with her family, she enjoys singing, playing the guitar, and exploring small, unsuspecting towns where people have no idea how accident-prone she is.

Find Christy online at: **www.christybarritt.com**

Sign up for Christy's newsletter to get information on all of her latest releases here: **www.christybarritt. com/newsletter-sign-up/**

facebook.com/AuthorChristyBarritt
instagram.com/cebarritt